1

I've known I was gay since I was thirteen. Does that surprise you? It didn't me.

According to one of the lousy books I read back then, I'm supposed to tell you it came as some sort of huge shock that sent me into fits of suicidal depression. Actually, it was the most natural thing in the world. I thought everyone was. At least until I hit high school the next year. That's when I finally realized all those faggot and dyke stories referred to people like me.

It was also about that time that I bumped into a half dozen guys whose idea of fun was to go out "queer bashing" on the weekend. Believe me, when I found out that meant they headed down to the park and pounded on someone who wasn't macho enough for them, I decided to go so deep into my closet that I'd probably still be there if it weren't for Paul. I mean, I'm a fairly easy-going guy but seeing him like that flipped me out. I never knew I could get mad enough to kill.

Maybe I'd better back up a minute and tell you who I am. Nance, that is Nancy Carrington, Paul's sister, always says I get ahead of myself in a story.

I'm Neil Meislich and you already know I'm gay. Before you go stereotyping me though, you should also know I'm nineteen, fullback on the school soccer team, a racing pigeon flyer, and an aspiring biologist. I plan to be famous in molecular genetics. I'm also interested in the martial arts and hold a black belt in a fighting style of kung-fu. I have one younger brother, Phil.

Physically, well, I don't want to seem vain but I'm not a bad looking guy. I'm 5'8", and 145 lbs. I do think my nose is too big but Paul always tells me I'm crazy. Besides, he says if I wear my hair over my ears, my nose doesn't seem to take up quite as much space. My hair's dark but I've got my dad's light skin. Phil takes after my mom, who's dead by the way. She died of cancer when I was eleven. That means Phil can tan all summer. I just tend to stroke. Since the summer here in Claremont can get to 110° that's not necessarily such an exaggeration either.

My dad's not a bad guy. He's a mechanic and a pretty good one. My brother takes after him. Me? When it comes to machinery I'm an absolute klutz. I can blow out a city's power supply simply by changing a light bulb. Dad always says he hopes I make it rich, if only to pay the repair bills on stuff I screw up.

When he found out I was gay there was an *adjustment* period, but he seemed to take it well, which is more than can be said for Paul's dad.

Paul's mom was no problem. She's nice enough but something of a knee-jerk liberal. She's for whatever's in that year. If Paul had told her last year when she was into the ecology movement she'd probably have hit the roof. His dad did hit it and didn't come down until — well, let me start at the beginning.

8

ALL-AMERICAN BOYS

All-American Boys

Frank Mosca

Alyson Publications, Inc. • Boston

First edition, first printing: September 1983.
second printing: March 1988.

Published as a trade paperback original by
Alyson Publications, Inc.
40 Plympton Street
Boston, Massachusetts 02118
Distributed in the U.K. by GMP Publishers
PO Box 247, London, N15 6RW, England

ISBN 0-932870-44-9

To Aaron La Barge, for literally dozens of reasons
but the best of which is he's my friend
and for that I'm very happy.

2

It was my day off work and I was lying around on the front lawn. I was watching a woodpecker search for bugs in the eucalyptus tree next door. Just then Brian Newton sauntered by.

"Hiya Neil. Watching those cruddy birds again?"

"Yeah. It's an acorn woodpecker." It's amazing how well I can keep the boredom out of my voice when I have to talk to him. That takes so much skill sometimes I should get an Oscar. Brian's personality makes a flatworm seem like interesting company.

He sprawled down beside me, but I lucked out. He sat downwind. I don't think he takes a shower more than twice a month, and he usually reeks of stale pot, sweat, and whatever.

"Why did you do that?" I asked as he winged a rock into the tree and scared the bird.

"I've got some news for you and I don't want you gawking at some stupid woodpecker."

"*You* don't want me." I guess my voice got a bit cold because he started backtracking fast.

"I mean, I figured you'd be more interested in knowing one foxy lady is moving in around the corner."

9

"Oh?"

"Yeah. She's moving into the empty place over on 12th. The one the cops raided last year. Want to go over?" He stood up. "We can check it out together. I only caught a quick look."

I laid there about five seconds thinking it over. Sure I was interested. It's so dead in this town that unless you have a car and can escape to Los Angeles, the big thrill is walking up and down the shopping center watching the plants die in the smog.

We rounded the corner just in time to see a guy land on his back under a sofa that was half in and half out of a U-Haul trailer.

"You okay?" I asked as I sprinted over to help him up.

"Sure. Thanks." He looked up at his help who was laughing his head off. He started to say something then began laughing himself.

I guess I looked bewildered because he turned to me and said, "The hyena on the trailer is my brother, Jeff. He thinks he's a comic, but he owed me one. I embedded all his underwear in a pail of Jello the other night."

"Oh." Notice how I'm always ready with a snappy comeback. But what do you say to something like that? I felt as if I'd just walked through the looking glass.

Brian came up. He startled me. I'd honestly forgotten about him. It's such an easy thing to do, he'd probably make a great spy.

"Who's your friend?" he asked.

I stifled a laugh. I could almost hear his busy little mind clicking, meet the guys and meet the girl.

"Well, the guy in the trailer's Jeff. This is his brother."

"Hi. I'm Paul Carrington."

He had a nice smile, I noticed.

"Neil Meislich. This is Brian Newton, a guy I know from school." I may be polite, but I had no intention of introducing Brian as a friend.

Jeff hopped down from the trailer. He was maybe an inch taller than his brother and about three taller than me. We went through the handshakes.

"Come on, you guys. Would you get that stuff into the house so dad can take the trailer back?"

Paul turned around.

"My sister, Nancy," he said to me. "And resident slavedriver." He looked over his shoulder to her.

I hate to admit it but Brian was right. She was good looking, 5'6", long brown hair.

"Slavedriver, maybe. But get that stuff into the house, will you? It's getting late." She watched as they took the sofa in, then turned and introduced herself. We went through the formalities again. I didn't think Brian was ever going to let go of her hand. From the look of boredom in her eyes, I'm sure she didn't think so either.

By the time Brian finally realized he was being ridiculous and released his grip, Jeff and Paul had come back out and were busy grabbing the last of the furniture.

"Hey, Neil. Would you mind taking that lamp in?" Paul asked. He nodded to one on the ground. "I can't grab anything else."

"Sure."

I followed him in. The place was the same as mine. That's the trouble with living in a tract, no surprises. Someday I'm going to be able to afford having an architect design a house for me and not Mr. Average Individual with his 2.3 kids. I think something with a sunken bar area and no right angles would be nice.

Paul dumped his armload in one of the bedrooms then walked back out smiling and said, "You're welcome to stay for lunch if you'd like. I know my folks won't mind.''

"Thanks, but I've just eaten. Besides, I guess I should be heading home.''

He shrugged.

"Okay. But that's an open invitation anytime you'd like.''

I picked Brian up as I left, but I was thinking about Paul. He really was a good looking guy and seemed pleasant enough. A little skinny maybe but... A shame he seemed to be such a kook.

It was a while before I heard Brian mumbling and realized he was talking to me.

"...don't you think so?''

"Huh?'' I really wish I could be like Juan. He's always got a snappy comeback ready.

"I said, she's pretty but probably a snob.''

"What's the matter?'' I asked dryly. "Doesn't she want to hop into bed with you?''

"I didn't say that.''

I just groaned. Brian is absolutely sure he's so attractive every girl in town is after him. The "Sex Symbol of Claremont High'' is the way he once described himself. Now I know everyone is entitled to a fantasy or two, but good lord!

I finally got rid of him when he left to go shoot a few baskets. The thing that amazed me about him is that for someone who was such a nut he actually had fairly decent taste in women. Personally, I found Paul a lot more attractive than Nancy. As beautiful as her hair was, I'd have preferred to tangle my fingers in his. And those calves. I'd noticed them when he bent to pick up the furniture. He looked like he'd done quite a bit of biking or running. I found myself thinking about him an awful lot the next few days.

3

I'd just finished putting the feed in for the pigeons and was heading out of the loft when I heard someone coming in the gate.

"Hi, Neil. I didn't know you were a flyer," Paul said as he walked in wearing a T-shirt and cut-off jeans. He looked up at the flock circling low over the house. "That red pied on the left is straggling a bit."

I stood there with my mouth open. Not only did he know the breed, he even called the hen right. Most people can't tell a pigeon from a crow let alone pick a lagging homer out of the flock.

"Yeah." I finally said. "She hurt her wing on a wire last week, but she's coming along fine. You a pigeon man?"

"Not really. My neighbor had racers and I spent some time over there. I used to take care of them while she was on vacation."

"Hang on a second while I get these things in and we can talk."

He stood back as I whistled and the birds began trapping in.

"I just stopped by to see if you might be interested in taking in a movie tonight," he said as the last of the birds pushed through the bob wires. "There's a new kung-fu flick playing downtown."

"Damn. It sounds good but I'm stuck working tonight. I'm on from five till ten." I tossed the feed can back into the bin. "By the way, how did you know where I lived?"

"I asked Brian. He's been making a pest of himself around the house with Nance but she's too polite to tell him to get lost." He blushed suddenly. "I'm sorry. I know he's a friend of yours but..."

"Don't worry about it. He's only an acquaintance, and you're right. He can be a pain."

Phil stuck his head out the bedroom window just then.

"Telephone, Neil. It sounds like Chuck. Something about an exhibition at the plaza." He vanished again.

"Be back in a minute," I said. "You're welcome to look over the youngsters in the first section but please stay out of the old bird section. Some of the breeders are pretty skittish."

When I got back Paul was in the loft. I watched him for a minute before I went over. Damn, but he had beautiful legs. I suddenly felt myself blushing. I didn't want to get too excited and be embarrassed if he turned around so I concentrated on his bird handling. There's no mistaking the touch. He had worked with pigeons before.

"Find any you like?" I asked looking through the dowels.

He turned and smiled. He really did have a nice smile, I noticed again.

"A few. That blue," he said pointing to one out of my best racing pair. "And that checker on the perch in the corner."

14

"You've just picked two of my best youngsters. Sure you've never flown before?"

"No. But my neighbor was a pretty good flyer and I picked up a lot from her. These are a nice stud of birds. They've all got nice egg-shaped bodies and loads of pectoral muscle."

"Thanks. I've been working with them since I was eleven. I think I'm finally getting my own family together."

Paul stepped out of the loft and latched the door.

"One suggestion," he said. "Why don't you see about closing the front of the loft so you can keep a more even temperature in there day and night? It helps the birds stay in top form. Shame about the movie, maybe another time."

I felt lost for a second. The conversation shift was too fast. Then I caught up.

"Yeah. Maybe next time. Thanks anyway."

Paul looked at his watch.

"I better leave. You've probably got to get ready for work." He was halfway out of the yard when he turned back and said, "By the way, that dinner invitation is still open."

To this day I don't know why I said anything. Maybe it was his smile. I'm a sucker for a cute smile.

"How about next Saturday?"

He looked surprised but recovered fast.

"Sure! Want to eat at my place or go out? It's on me."

"There's a good Japanese restaurant about eight miles from here."

"Sounds good to me. I'll give you a call Saturday morning and we can decide on the time. What's your number?"

"It's in the book under G. Aaron Meislich."

"Okay, see you Saturday then."

All I can remember about the next three days is a horde of swearing customers. Two of the pumps were out again and the gas company had raised its prices. The way those people were screaming at me, you'd have thought I owned the wells and was purposely cutting back production.

If I hadn't needed the money so bad for college next year, I'd have told the boss to stuff it. I stood out there taking all the crud and he sat in the office taking six hours to do the bookwork. Anyone else could do it in two, even with time out to service cars.

I was so exhausted Friday night when I got home that I skipped supper. I just kind of grunted to Dad as I collapsed on the floor in the living room. As tired as I was, I was too tense to go to bed immediately so I scrounged up the sports section and paged absently through it. Dad was half-heartedly watching the news.

I crumpled up the paper and rolled to my feet, then stopped still as the announcer began talking about the Gay Freedom Parade in Los Angeles. Dad grunted sourly as a picture of a heavily bearded man dressed as the good fairy flashed on the screen.

"I have a lot of trouble understanding stuff like that," he said.

I kept quiet.

We watched as the cameras panned across thousands of men and women, some in costume, most in jeans.

"You know," I finally said, "we had a couple of speakers who were gay show up in class last year."

"What did you think of them?" he asked casually.

I chose my words carefully. I don't like to lie.

"Okay, I guess. I really got to understand some of the garbage they've got to put up with." I watched his face closely as he nodded.

"I suppose so. But you have to admit they bring a lot

16

of it on themselves. I don't care what they do so long as they don't keep throwing it in my face. I don't hate them. I just don't like them."

He pointed at the TV which was showing a float full of muscular men dancing happily with their shirts off.

"Look. That's what I mean."

I was wishing I had known about it, I might have gotten a ride into town. No one would know me in that crowd, and those men were sure handsome.

"Maybe they're just having fun," I finally suggested lamely. "They look like they're having a good time. That's not so bad, is it? I remember one speaker said he'd never been able to hold his date's hand until he was twenty-eight. That seems kind of sad."

Dad shrugged and reached for the front page of the paper. "Why are you so interested anyway?"

My mouth went dry, and I thought this might be the moment, but instead I said, "Just hate to see anyone kicked around." I yawned. "I better get some sleep."

I kicked myself all the way down the hall. My hands were clenched so tight my nails nearly bit into my palm. Why didn't I just tell him I thought I might be gay?

I crawled into bed and stared at the ceiling wondering what he would do if I told him — would he love me, or what? Exhaustion finally took over. Even Phil's snores didn't keep me awake. The last thing I remember wondering as I fell asleep was what he was doing in bed at 11:30 on a Friday night. Usually, he was out partying.

4

Five-thirty the next morning I found out what he had been doing in bed so early. Phil's a good kid, but quiet he ain't. I ignored the first two or three slamming drawers. But who can possibly ignore a blaring stereo, even with a pillow and two blankets over his head?

"What are you doing?" I asked as I popped my head out from under the covers, and just as promptly stuffed it back under again. The sun was starting to creep into the room and it was blinding me.

"Getting ready to go trout fishing."

"Can't you do it a bit more quietly?"

"I am being quiet."

Unfortunately, he was also being honest. For Phil, slamming drawers and a stereo screaming is fairly quiet. Usually, he sounds like a herd of elephants feeding or the fans at the Super Bowl when someone's scored.

"Oh. Well, would you turn the stereo down a few hundred decibels more, please?" I poked my head back out. I can't be sure since my eyes wouldn't quite focus yet, but I think he looked as if I'd suggested murdering his favorite rock star.

"Down?"

When I nodded, he reluctantly lowered the sound. Not enough to make any difference but he did do it and for him that was quite a concession.

"Thank you." I burrowed back under my pillow. "And please shut it off when you leave."

Twenty minutes later things settled down again. Settled down, that is, for the thirty seconds it took him to get from the room to his car. It's street legal — but just barely. The motor has a gentle hum, sort of like that produced by a twin-engine Cessna passing over at thirty feet. I gave up and crawled out of bed as the purr of the motor faded into the distance.

Five minutes later I was standing out by the loft releasing the birds. It was gorgeous. No smog yet, and cool before the day's heat picked up. The birds climbed to about three hundred feet and set out for somewhere. When they move like that I know they won't be home for at least an hour. I changed the water and put out a bath pan for them. There's nothing a pigeon likes better than splashing around in the water after a flight.

There's also nothing I like better than lounging around so I sprawled on the chaise and soaked up some of the early morning sun. I suppose I fell asleep because the next thing I knew Bombs Away was perched on my chest and pecking at my lips. She's one of two birds I had to hand rear in the house when a Cooper's hawk picked off their mother. Phil named her for reasons which are probably apparent.

"Morning, Neil."

Bombs Away flew back to the bath pan. I looked around and there was Paul dressed in a pair of blue cutoffs and what had to be the most outrageous print shirt I've ever seen. It was a great blending of purple, green, yellow, red, and a few other colors I wouldn't even guess at.

"Hi, Paul. What are you doing up so early?"

"I'm always up early. I spotted the birds heading over so I decided to stop by and see about tonight rather than calling. I didn't know if everyone was up or just you."

"Everyone's probably up by now, but thanks. It was considerate of you to worry about it. Uh, by the way, where did you get that shirt?"

He looked down at it, over at me, then grinned broadly.

"Hideous, isn't it? My dad got it for me back in Illinois just before we moved. He was sure it was what everyone in California wore and he wanted me to fit right in. He meant well." His eyebrows lifted. "Besides, I love it. It's so atrocious."

I cracked up. He laughed too and flopped down into the chair beside me.

"So. What do you have planned for today?" he asked.

"Not much, really. I'll be heading down to the kung-fu studio in a bit to work out, then nothing."

"That's right. Brian did say something about you being into that. Isn't it dangerous, though? I mean busting boards and stuff?"

"I've never even cracked a knuckle on a board, except one time when I showed a new kid the trick to doing it."

"No?"

"Nope. Just think. When was the last time you were attacked by a wild board, or even a tame one?"

He looked at me as if I were insane.

"All I'm saying," I continued, "is that it's dumb to bust boards when people are the danger. We learn to fight people."

"How come you got into kung-fu?"

I smiled a bit grimly as I remembered.

"I could tell you it was love of the art, but the fact is,

I spent a good portion of my time in grade school getting the snot kicked out of me by almost everyone.

"The last time it happened Dad decided I was going to learn to defend myself. He didn't have time to teach me to box so he took me down to the kung-fu school and signed me up."

I shrugged.

"Since then I've grown to love it. I like being able to make my body do what I want, when I want."

"Would you mind if I tagged along and watched you work out today?"

"Not if you don't mind sitting around for a few hours." I was a bit afraid he might decide not to.

"I don't mind. I don't have any plans either."

I don't *think* I let my breath out audibly.

5

Five minutes later we were heading downtown. I found out Paul was also going to be a senior the coming year. He was considering a career in law, aeronautics, computer research, business, foreign service, or consumer protection. As he put it, "Whatever I happen to be crazy about this weekend."

His family had moved to Claremont so Nancy could go to school here. After all, we do have five of the country's top colleges in town. His folks figured since she wanted to go to Pitzer and they wanted to get out of the cold, it was a great excuse to pack up and leave.

Paul was absolutely fantastic. One second, one subject, and then the next something from left field. The amazing thing was he was interesting. I've never met anyone who knew so much and yet was so willing to admit when he knew nothing about a subject.

Talk about politics, he knew who was voting for what. Talk about soccer, he was up on the team standings. Talk about the space program, he was presenting valid arguments for keeping it alive. He was even more than layman knowledgeable about facets of molecular genetics, especially cloning. I was so caught up by him, I nearly drove by the studio, and I've been going there four times a week for the last four years.

"Is that your instructor?" he asked as I parked.

I looked over to where he was pointing and saw Chuck unlocking the front door for some students.

"Sure is. Come on, I'll introduce you."

"Morning, Neil," Chuck said as we came up.

"Morning. I'd like you to meet a friend of mine, Paul Carrington."

"Interested in kung-fu, Paul?" Chuck asked as they shook.

"Not really. I just came down to watch Neil work out."

"You should enjoy it. Neil's one of my better students."

They both looked at me.

I could feel myself starting to blush. When I blush I don't fool around. Ketchup bottle kid they call me at school. I was embarrassed but I can't honestly say I was upset. Chuck doesn't hand out compliments too often. As far as I'm concerned, one from him is worth five from anyone else.

"Excuse me," I mumbled, "I'd better get my *gi* on."

I headed for the dressing room. I kicked the bag so hard as I walked by that it bashed into the wall. I knew why I was so hyper. It was only a Saturday workout, but the way I felt you would have thought I was getting ready to take my test for the next belt grade.

I wished I could tell someone how I felt. I didn't think Dad or Phil would understand, assuming I had the guts to tell them, and Paul would probably choke if I told him he had great legs and a smile that made me want to grab him and hang on for hours.

Five of the guys were dressing out. Unfortunately, one of them was Danny Mello. Juan was there too, and Juan's great. I really like the guy. How can you not like someone who's slightly insane?

Last year, for example, he and a few of his friends got together and cooked up a "murder." They all met at the K-Mart parking lot and started a fight. The yelling got louder until finally one of them pulled a knife he'd borrowed from the school theater prop department and stabbed Juan. Juan fell, squirting fake blood all over the place. His friends picked him up, threw him into the back of their van and took off. Ten minutes later they were back in different cars. Juan even had the gall to go over to one of the cops and give his own description as the victim.

Naturally, within a few hours the police figured out what had happened. They lectured Juan and his buddies up and down. I found out from a girl in my trig class whose dad is on the force, though, that they all thought it was hysterical.

I was totally hyper as I dressed out and I put my belt on wrong. I haven't done that since my first week there. I didn't even hear Juan talking to me until he threw a jab at my shoulder and connected. I'm supposed to be alert enough to block stuff like that but I didn't even see it coming. Juan looked surprised. It was the first time he'd tagged me in weeks.

"Slow. Too slow," he said in mock disgust. Then he leered. "I know what it is," he said. "You were out partying last night. Was she cute?"

"Who?"

He slipped into his street Chicano accent — something he only does when he's pulling your leg.

"Oh, man. You know. I mean the one you were out with last night. Come on, man. Don't lie to me. I know all

24

about these Anglo chicks. They're pretty good. I mean like, I've heard the stories. They true, man? Can a poor low-class guy from the *barrio* make it with one?''

"*Barrio!* Hell, the closest you've ever come to the *barrio* is scrounging a taco off the lunch wagon. As for low-class, well, personally I agree with you, but your dad makes more in a year than mine makes in two.''

He looked crushed. "Oh no, man. My dad. You know what I mean. He's only a garbage collector. And my mom. You know my mom. She works ten, twelve hours a day doing laundry from those dirty *gavachos* and. . .''

That's when I threw a kick at him that he blocked easily. His dad happens to be head of the school board in town and his mom's a salesclerk at the *Broadway*.

"You do know you're insane," I said.

"That's the trouble with you scientific types," he said as he dropped the accent. "You deal in facts. Let's go stretch out.''

Paul smiled as I walked onto the floor and I waved.

I grabbed Juan while Chuck went back to prepare the first lesson.

"Want to work out for a few minutes?" I asked.

"Sure.''

"Ah, mind if we get a little flamboyant? There's a friend of mine here," I said nodding in Paul's direction, "and he's never seen a workout before.''

For a split second I thought I saw something flash in Juan's eyes but then he said, "Okay. But watch the left arm, will you? It's a little sore.''

He backed off and suddenly launched a right roundhouse kick at my head. I parried it, came up low under his groin with my right arm and took him to the floor. I got him with a heel to the solar plexus and a hammer to the head. We broke and stood up. This time he came in low and tried to sweep my legs out. He nearly got me, too. We've studied together for so long he knows my weak points.

I'm afraid I really got carried away. Instead of going for something simple like a return sweep while he was off balance, I flaunted it. I kicked him to the stomach and as he bent forward in simulated agony — we always react to a pulled punch as if it were real — I leaped on him from the front. I brought him over with me as I rolled to the floor and landed with him on the bottom.

"Ham!" he hissed softly as I stood up.

It was my turn to attack so I lashed out with a backfist. He stopped it easily and contented himself with a basic armlock and takedown.

Just then Chuck walked back in. He demonstrated the lesson and I forgot about Paul as I helped a yellow belt student. We took it slow and he finally got it.

Juan didn't seem to be having as much luck. He'd gotten stuck with Danny Mello, who's one of those types whose mouth is always going on about how great the rest of his body is. What's worse is he's always trying to correct what someone else is doing right.

Juan looked over at me as he turned from the sight of Danny botching a basic block for the third time in a row and he shrugged. I just smirked.

The morning went quickly. Paul was waiting for me as I stepped out of the dressing room.

"You're pretty good," he said as we headed for the car.

"Thanks. But I've still got quite a way to go before I'm near as good as Chuck or some of the others here. Besides," I said as I felt myself blushing a bit, "I was hamming it up a bit this morning."

"Oh," he said wryly. "I hadn't noticed." He looked at me and we both laughed, but I could feel myself blushing deeper. I glanced down at his legs and started quivering a bit as I suddenly thought of them pressed against me. Then I looked in his eyes. I felt like they were looking right through me, and I was sure he realized what I was thinking about. I nearly apologized verbally for thinking he was handsome beyond belief.

"I'm starved," I said almost desperately. "Want to stop for a taco or something? It's on me."

"Sounds good. But don't forget I promised you dinner tonight."

"I haven't. And I'll warn you, I'm crazy about Japanese food."

All the way over I tried to keep my mind on my driving but Paul made it so difficult. I wanted so much to know everything about him. I was shaking, trying hard to be casual but I wanted to reach over and take his hand, just to touch him. God, how I wanted to touch him, and I couldn't.

I missed what he said at one point because I was frantically trying to remember what one of the books I'd read had said about situtions like these. I realized with sudden anguish they had all assumed you'd been open about yourself for years. None of them told me how to tell someone you were gay and crazy about them all at once. Especially not someone as good looking and articulate as Paul.

6

I pulled into the *Mi Taco* by the freeway and drove up to the mike.

"How does a Coke and burrito sound?" I asked Paul.

"Like a flute?"

"Huh?"

"Sorry," he said softly as he scratched the back of his neck. "I forget you don't know my sense of humor yet. What's a burrito?"

"You've never had one?"

He shook his head.

"It's a flour tortilla wrapped around refried beans, meat, cheese, and whatever. There are tons of ways of making them. They're not bad."

"Sounds okay with me then."

I ordered, picked it up, then drove to an empty space near the edge of the lot.

"Well, now that I've got it what do I do with it?" He shifted it around in his hands looking for a place to bite.

"Take it from the top. There's hot sauce in the bag if you want it."

"I'm willing to try anything once." He poured the

sauce over the burrito he was strangling in a death grip. Some of the beans and melted cheese squirted out the bottom of the wrapped tortilla and began oozing down his bare leg.

"Ah, Neil. I think I've done something wrong." He scooped the gloop onto one finger and stuck it into his mouth. "Doesn't taste bad though."

"Trick number one, don't squeeze so hard. Number two, just unwrap enough for one bite."

We sat there eating in silence for a minute or two. Then he turned to me and said, "Well, now that you're full and all exercised, are you mellow too?"

Something in his voice, a quaver of anxiety that hadn't been there before, made me pause in the middle of my last sip of Coke. I looked at him. He scratched the back of his neck and he blushed slightly.

"You know," he said, "I've done this twice before so you'd think it would be easier this time. But hell, it's worse."

"What are you talking about, Paul?"

"Look, Neil. You seem like a hell of a nice guy . . ."

"Thanks. So do you, but—" He held out his hand to stop me.

"Let me finish."

I noticed his hand was shaking.

"I know I'm being melodramatic. It's a fault but I've got to say this my own way."

"Okay."

"Look, Neil. I don't make friends too easily. Acquaintances sure, but not friends. And you really seem like someone I'd like to have as a friend. As far as I'm concerned though a friend is someone you don't have to play word games with. Someone you can be yourself around without having to be on stage all the time. Someone you don't have to lie to."

29

"All right, I'll give you that," I said. "I think so too, but what in heaven—"

He stopped me again, bit his lip, then said, "Neil. If what I tell you bothers you, let me know and I'll split. I mean I never know when to tell someone. If I tell them after I get to know them I feel like we've never known each other. But if I tell them first I may never get to know them so I'm not sure."

I kept myself from screaming as I asked, "What are you talking about?" — but only just barely.

"I'm not being noble or anything. It's just that I was hurt too much once before by someone I thought was a friend and I couldn't hack that again. She was... well anyway. What I'm trying to tell you is that I'm gay. Homosexual if you prefer. I used to go over to a gay group at the college near my home in Illinois."

For a second I just sat there. I felt as if the car had exploded.

"You're queer!" I yelled as I spilled what was left of my Coke down my leg. His grab for the door and the sudden pain in his eyes made me realize the asinine thing I'd done.

"Wait," I said as I grabbed his shoulder and literally yanked him back. He tried to shrug me off. "I'm sorry, Paul. I can't tell you how sorry. Really I am." I prayed to whatever gods were around that I could make amends. "It was a reflex. A stupid, asinine reflex."

He sat watching me, wary but not trying to pull away any more. His breathing was shallow and he kept tugging at his chin with his left hand.

"I mean, hell, I'm..." Suddenly I felt my throat constrict and a cold sweat break out all over me. I couldn't do it. Seventeen years of lies, of practiced hiding, and of fear caught up with me in one stupefying second. I wanted to cry out with rage, and I couldn't even do that. The books I'd read had never said anything about this. They'd said it might be difficult, not impossible.

Suddenly it seemed to get darker, and the car closed in on me. My throat constricted and only Paul existed for me. His eyes narrowed as he looked at me. I was shaking so hard the hand I grabbed Paul with was bouncing him around like there was an earth tremor. I could feel the words I wanted to say in my mouth but they wouldn't come out. My skin was clammy.

"What's wrong, Neil?" Paul asked worriedly. "You suddenly went pale as a ghost. Are you all right?"

I tried again but still nothing came out.

"Damn it, Neil!" he yelled. "Snap out of it. Are you okay or do you need a doctor?" He turned and started to bolt from the car.

I clamped down on his shoulder again and fought to get control of myself.

"No," I stammered. "It's okay. It's just that, well..." I blurted it out all in one breath, "so am I."

He stared at me.

"So am I what?" he asked suspiciously.

"Gay." I whispered it. I could feel the tension starting to drain away. It was like someone pulled a plug. "But I've never told anyone that before. No one! I don't even know another gay person."

He simply stared at me.

"You mean, I've been going crazy for the last few days trying to figure out the right way to tell you and you're gay?"

I nodded and started to grin nervously. I still didn't really believe it. I'd actually done it. I'd told someone. After all those years of lying and hiding.

"Yeah," I said. "I've been really trying to get up the nerve for the last few months to stop in at one of the meetings they have here in Claremont. I couldn't. Damn, I'd get as far as the street it was on, drive around the block, then go home and sit in my bedroom kicking myself for having no guts.

"Then I thought maybe it would be easier in Los Angeles. I even got as far as the front door at the Gay and Lesbian Community Services Center down there before I chickened out. I went to a *sushi* bar nearby instead."

He still stared. "I don't believe it."

"You know," I said, "I've spent the last few days imagining how it would be if *you* were gay."

He started to laugh. I started laughing too. In three seconds we were both roaring so loud we must have looked like maniacs because we got strange looks from people in the other cars. Finally, I managed to catch my breath, but I was holding my side.

"Let's get out of here," I said.

7

"I don't think Dad needs the car and I don't really feel like sitting around the house," I said as we headed back. "You want to take in a movie or something? Maybe that kung-fu flick if it's still playing?"

"Sounds like a winner to me."

"Okay. But let me stop somewhere and get this Coke off me first."

The theater was jammed with kids, which was fun. It gave us a chance to talk without upsetting anyone. Besides, no one paid any attention when we went crazy screaming for the good guys.

"I've got one more confession to make," Paul said suddenly as we were heading home.

"Now what? I don't think my nervous system can take many more today."

"It's just that I've been sort of pumping Brian about you. I didn't say anything about being gay, but I was hoping he might know if you were. At the very least, I was hoping he could tell me what kind of a guy you were. You're not upset, are you?"

"Hell, no. I'm flattered you went through so much

trouble." Just then I spotted Dad standing in the driveway. "Damn. I bet he needed the car after all."

"Your dad?"

"Yeah."

"Where have you been since noon?" Dad asked as we got out.

"At the movies. Why? Did you need the car for something?"

"I had hoped to pick up an alternator at the shop and they close in fifteen minutes." He stood there looking irritated. He's very good at looking irritated. He used to be a sergeant in the Army.

"We can probably make it down there if you want us to get it for you," I offered.

He thought about that for a minute, then relaxed.

"No. Don't worry about it. I can pick it up tomorrow. Besides," he said smiling, "I don't feel like putting it in today anyway." He turned and headed for the house. "But in the future," he said turning back, "would you please remember to call if you're going to disappear for awhile?"

"Sure, Dad. Sorry."

We followed him into the house.

"Do I know you?" he said to Paul.

"I don't think so, Mr. Meislich. I'm Paul Carrington. I moved into the area about a week ago."

"Glad to meet you. Oh, and Neil. That spaced out kid was here looking for you a few times this afternoon."

"Spaced out?"

"Yeah. The one with the stringy hair who needs a bath."

"Brian Newton?"

He nodded. "He was looking for a basketball game or something. He wants you to call. But there's no rush. I told him you might be busy for a week or so."

Paul tried to keep from laughing and lost.

"He must work fast," Dad said. "You're only here a week and you've been bored by him too?"

"Yes, sir. He's been hanging around my sister."

Dad looked at him. "You have my sympathies. All I can suggest is a can or two of *Raid* and maybe some *Lysol*."

"On that note," I said snickering, "I'm going to get ready for tonight."

"I think I'll head home myself," Paul said.

"Like me to run you over?"

"No thanks. I'll walk."

"Okay. I'll see you in about twenty minutes or so."

Nancy looked up from where she was kneeling near some newly planted yuccas when I got there.

"Hi, Neil. Paul said you'd be over. Just go on in, the door's open."

"Thanks. Hey, we're planning to have supper. Would you like to go along?"

She looked at me quizzically. "No thanks. Paul would strangle me."

"Strangle you. Why?"

"No reason. We just have a firm policy about not doing too many things together. It helps keep us off each other's nerves." She smiled and so did I, though I wasn't quite sure at what.

I walked in and was spread out on the floor reading *Broom Hilde* in the *Times* when I heard someone walk up behind me. I looked and there was Paul's mom standing there with a watering can. It was easy to see where Nancy got her hair.

"Hi, Mrs. Carrington." I scrambled somewhat embarrassedly to my feet. I feel if you're caught on someone's living room floor for the first time, you should at least be looking at the editorial section and not the comics.

"I'm Neil Meislich. Nancy said to come on in."

"That's fine, Neil. I'm glad to meet you. Paul's been talking about you all week." She put her watering can on the TV. "I'm glad he's met someone here. He doesn't make friends too easily."

"He's a nice guy."

She smiled. Nancy may have gotten her hair, but Paul sure got her smile.

"Excuse me," she said. "I have to finish getting my plants watered, then I have to get some shopping done. You make yourself comfortable."

I watched as she picked up the can, sprinkled her way around the room, and then out.

"All set?" Paul asked as he walked in.

"Sure am." I threw the paper on the coffee table as we left.

"What do you want to do after suppper?" he asked as I started the car.

"Nothing in particular."

"Is there anyplace around here we can go dancing?"

"Sure, but I don't know where I can get hold of any girls on such short notice."

"Who said anything about women?"

"You mean just us?" I was stunned.

"Of course."

"God. I don't know."

"You mean you've never gone dancing with another guy?"

"Of course not. I told you this was all new to me. I've heard there's a few gay spots in Garden Grove and San Bernardino but I'm not sure where."

"Can't we check with that center you mentioned in Los Angeles?"

"I guess so, but even if they can tell us do you think we can get in?"

"How old are you?"

"Seventeen. Why?"

"Most places have at least an 18-year-old limit."

"I won't make that until next month."

"I made it two months ago," he said.

"We could always head down to Chino and look for the Green Mist."

"The what?"

"Green Mist," I explained. "You sometimes see the stuff outside of town in the hills. The official explanation is that car lights shine off the ground fog, but I don't buy that. Stories about it go back to way before cars. Some of them are pretty weird, people vanishing and all. There's even one about a guy who left his girl in the car so he could get help when they broke down. They're supposed to have found him the next morning hanging by his heels with his throat slit."

"You are kidding, I hope."

"That's the story, though I have to admit I've only heard it fourteenth hand."

I pulled into the restaurant lot.

"We can decide after supper," I said. "I hope you like *sushi*. It's a house specialty."

"Never had it."

"No *sushi* and no burritos. Boy, you *have* led a deprived life."

"I've got my charm and wit to keep me happy. Who needs food?" He smiled. "What's *sushi*?"

"Basically, it's vinegared rice shaped into little pats and topped with raw fish and a horseradish called *wasabi* that will lift the hair on the back of your head. Sometimes they chop it with seaweed, or eggs, or anything."

He looked at me in horror. "Raw fish. You're sick!!"

"No. It's really good."

"If that's all this place serves, I'll watch you eat."

37

"You can always have the *tempura*. They make it great."

"What's that?" He sounded suspicious.

"It's anything dipped into a batter and fried."

"Cooked?"

"Oh yeah."

"Thank god," he said fervently.

I ordered the *sushi* special. Paul got the *tempura*.

"Are you really going to eat that?" he asked as I popped a tuna into my mouth.

I nodded and chewed.

"It is pretty, I have to admit. It doesn't look like fish."

"I know," I said swallowing. "The chef's an artist."

"I hate to ask since it's your dinner, but it does look good. Can I try one? Maybe one of those red things you ate."

"That's tuna. And try this one too. Most people prefer it to the tuna."

"Oh my god." He took half a bit and tears came into his eyes. "You weren't kidding about that horseradish. But nothing ventured . . . ."

He crammed the rest of the piece into his mouth.

"Actually, not bad," he gasped. "But a little mushy."

"Yeah. I happen to like it though. Try the other one. Even Phil likes that and he doesn't eat anything else."

"Now this ain't bad," he said as he chewed thoughtfully. "It's got more body to it. What is it?"

"Sure you want to know?"

He looked at me closely, then swallowed.

"Let me finish eating first. Here, have a couple of shrimp."

We got down to eating.

"By the way," I said, "Nancy claimed you'd strangle

her if she came along tonight. What was she talking about?''

He blushed and suddenly seemed to find something exceedingly interesting under a lettuce leaf on his plate.

''When you said you wanted to go out, I told her I was thrilled. Then today when I found out you were gay I told her if anything came up to stop tonight I'd probably kill.''

I felt as if an army of ants had just marched up my spine.

''Why, thank you. I'm really flattered.''

''Well, it's true.''

''That's why I'm flattered,'' I said. ''Nancy knows you're gay?''

''Yeah. But she's the only one in the family. When I came out I had to tell someone. I was going crazy trying to keep it inside. I'd finally found myself and I was thrilled. I mean, I knew who I was for the first time in my life. I didn't tell my folks because I didn't want them to think I was trying to hurt them. And I guess maybe because I'm a little scared.

''Scared?''

''Yeah. My dad's okay but he makes the right wing look liberal.''

I nodded.

''You do realize Nancy also knows about you? I told her when I got home.''

I paused. I wasn't too sure I liked the idea; I was still getting used to hearing it out loud myself.

''Okay. But just so long as it's only the two of you.''

''That's it. Now what was that last piece of *sushi* I ate?''

''*Tako.*''

''What's that? Some sort of fish?''

''No. It's a mollusk.''

39

"You mean like a clam or something?"

"Yeah. Only it doesn't have a shell." I was doing my best to spring it on him gradually. Some people have violent reactions.

"Not a slug!" His face had a greenish tinge.

"Of course not," I said indignantly. "I'd never do that to you." His face went back to pink. "It was octopus."

He looked relieved. "Is that all? I thought it was something lethal the way you were beating around the bush."

Maybe I'm rotten but I was disappointed he was taking it so calmly.

"You've had octopus before?"

"No. But my mom's Italian. I grew up on squid that was stuffed with breadcrumbs and thrown in the tomato sauce for the spaghetti."

"Then why were you so upset when I ordered the *sushi*?"

"At least my squid was cooked."

"Ask a dumb question... What about the rest of the evening?"

"Why not call that center and check out the dance places?"

"I'm not sure I'm ready for something like that yet."

"Scared?"

"Yeah. A little I think, and thrilled by the idea too."

"That's fine then," he said. "We—"

"What the hell," I broke in. "At least I can check."

I got back as he was handing the cashier the money.

"I can cover the tip," I told him.

"Nope. Not tonight. This one's on me all the way. Besides, you're paying for the gas."

"The guy at the center said there was a place in San Bernardino called The Junction but it's got an age limit.

So do the places in Garden Grove. I guess that leaves the beach or the mist or something."

Paul looked at me with a funny expression. "Let's forget the beach and go find us a ghost."

8

"Now what?" Paul asked as I guided the car off the road and into a patch of mixed scrub and weeds.

"Now we hike up that small access road over there to the top of the hill and check out the valley east of here. That's where I saw the mist the last time."

"Are you sure you want to go?" he asked. "I've been thinking about this. How true are those stories about people disappearing?"

"I don't know. Why? You scared?"

"Let's just say I never did like sticking my hand over a fence till I was sure there wasn't a dog on the other side."

"Come on. Chances are we won't even see it. I've been here dozens of times and only seen it once."

"Sure you weren't just high that night?"

"Come to think of it, no. But let's go anyway. Oh—" I couldn't resist saying as he opened the car door, 'If you hear any rattlers, don't move."

"Rattlers!" He grabbed the roof so fast his right leg swung up and almost hit the car window. "You are bull-shitting me I hope."

He looked so scared sitting there I had to stop.

"Yeah. I've only seen two up here in five years. They're more scared of us than we are of them."

"Don't you bet on it, you sadist." He relaxed enough to put his foot on the ground. He did look first though, I noted.

We picked our way up and over some rocks in the moonlight.

"Over there," I said pointing, "between that oak and the other hill. That's where I saw it the last time."

"Doesn't seem to be anything there now."

"Let's give it a half hour or so. Anyway, we've been running all day. This gives us a chance to sit and relax."

We sprawled out in a patch of dried mustard plants. He leaned back against my legs and I could feel the heat of his body through my pants. I ran my hand slowly through his hair and he squirmed back against me and rubbed my right shin. We sat quietly. I was afraid if I said anything he might move to answer me and I was feeling just fine about where he was.

The chirping of the night insects, the occasional shooting star, and Paul's presence more than made up for the lack of the mist. Especially Paul. I was in heaven. Even the sound of his breathing and the rustle of his shirt were beautiful.

"Look, Neil," he said, "a barn owl."

We watched the bird course along looking like a giant moth in the moonlight.

"I'm crazy about those birds," he went on. "We used to have a pair of them nesting in the garage back home."

Suddenly the bird's wings went straight over his back and he dropped, only to rise with what looked like clenched talons. We watched it fly off into the darkness.

"Neil." Paul's voice had some of that same tenseness he had at the taco stand. "Have I remembered to tell you that you're a hell of a nice guy?" He looked back over his shoulder and smiled shyly.

"No." I felt stunned.

"Well, you are. I wanted to let you know. I also happen to think you're one foxy-looking dude."

"Me?" My brain was racing so fast I barely noticed my hand jumping with each beat of my heart.

"Don't sound so surprised. Yeah, you."

"You mean physical type attractive?"

He laughed. "Of course, silly."

I was stunned again.

"God. I've never thought of myself as attractive. I mean, no one's ever said that to me before."

"Then they were stupid." He reached back and touched my face softly. "I love the way your hair curls over your forehead, and your arms. I saw you when you pulled your *gi* top off this morning. You've got great arms."

"I think you're kind of okay too. You're bright and more than a little fun to be around."

He touched my arm. Our kiss was gentle. As for what happened afterwards, well, there are parts of everyone's life that are not open for public inspection. I can tell you though, I loved every minute of it.

9

The next few weeks were heaven. I even cut down my trips to the studio to once a week. The more I saw of Paul, the more I wanted to see of him. Things were going so well, in fact, I didn't even mind looking up one afternoon while I was feeding the birds to see Brian's squirrelly little face pushed up against the dowels.

"Haven't seen much of you lately," he said.

"I've been busy."

"Seeing a lot of Paul, huh?" It was a friendly question but I felt uncomfortable.

"Yeah. Why?"

"You know he's a fag?"

Suddenly I felt the way I did when I lost every bird I sent to a smash race — kind of queasy sick and hyper all rolled into one.

"A what?" I stammered.

"A fag. Like in fruitcake."

"What the hell makes you say something like that?"

"Because it's true. My cousin's working at the school as a receptionist. She told me he came in trying to find out if they had a gay club on campus."

"Well, even if it's true, and I doubt it, what business is it of yours or your cousin's?"

"I just thought you might like to know. I mean, people talk. If you're around him enough they might begin to think your wrist isn't all that firm either. I know I'm sure not going over to his place anymore."

Something snapped then. I don't know what. Maybe it was because of his snotty attitude. I tossed the feed can down and walked out of the loft.

"Look, Brian," I said. "My friends are my friends. I don't care if they're straight, bi, gay, or get their jollies rubbing against pine trees in the spring. Clear? If anyone doesn't like it, he can shove it up his rosyred."

"Sure. But why are you suddenly so hostile? Or maybe you *do* have something to hide."

I swear his beady little eyes bulged then.

"Come to think of it," he sneered, "he sure asked an awful lot of questions about you when he first moved here. You maybe sprinkling your own share of fairy dust around, Tinkerbell?"

That did it. I moved behind him and locked out his arm and shoulder.

"Look, Brian." I applied some pressure to emphasize the point. "I'm going to tell you this once and once only. I don't like you. In fact, I've never liked you. You're an obnoxious individual, and what's worse you stink."

He grunted and tried to swing around to hit me. I moved with him and jammed his arm so hard he was trying to walk tiptoe.

"Furthermore, I don't ever want to see you again. Is that understood?" He grunted again. "What?"

"Yeah! Yeah!"

I pointed him toward the gate and released him.

"Get lost before I forget I'm basically a nice person and break your arm."

He walked slowly to the gate rubbing his shoulder as he went. "I always knew you were a fucking faggot," he yelled as he reached it.

I started over to kill him.

"I've seen you checking me out in the showers."

That was so ludicrous, I lost all interest in killing him and started laughing.

"Then you've got a hell of a memory," I managed to get out between laughs. "I've never showered with you. In fact, I don't think you've ever showered. Hell, you smell so rank I've seen turkey vultures backtracking downwind of you trying to find the corpse."

He kicked the fence and left. I watched him limp away. Thirty seconds later I was on the phone to Paul. Jeff answered.

"Is Paul around?" I snapped.

"No. He's down at the store picking up some stuff for Mom."

"Would you tell him I have to talk to him?"

"Sure. Is something the matter?"

"No. Why?"

"It's just that you usually say hello and don't sound so upset."

"I'm sorry. Nothing's wrong. But could you have Paul call me?"

"Sure."

Twenty-five aggravating minutes later, Paul knocked and walked in.

"Hi, Neil. What's up?"

"Are you absolutely out of your damned mind?" I snapped. "Or are you simply some basic moronic asshole?"

"Huh?" His smile faded and he looked as if I'd punched him.

"Did you really have to be so stupid as to walk into

47

the office at school and ask about a Gay Student Union? Shit! By now Brian's probably told half the school you're a queer and the other half probably suspects me."

He looked at me for a good five seconds. His left fist clenched and his eyes went blank.

"First off," he said coldly but calmly, "I am not queer. Not to you, not to anyone. I'm gay. Second, you mentioned something about a GSU in town and with school starting next week I was simply trying to find it."

"I meant at the colleges, not the high school."

"Third," he continued as if he hadn't heard me, "just who in hell do you think you are to jump all over me the second I walk in? If you want to play some weird macho trip, do it at the studio. I don't play games."

Without another word he turned and walked out.

I watched him leave, then threw a magazine halfway across the room. "Who gives a damn," I thought. "Let him go. At least I can salvage something out of the mess. With any luck I can apologize to Brian and...."

Suddenly I was furious with myself. Apologize to Brian?! Brian! I couldn't stomach Brian and I was more worried about him than about Paul.

I went flying out of the house and raced after Paul. I caught up to him at the corner, grabbed him by the shoulder, and spun him around.

He didn't say anything. He simply stared at my hand. I could feel myself blushing and released him.

"You have something to say?" he asked coldly. I could see he'd been crying.

"What can I say?" I asked softly.

"Try 'I'm sorry' to start with."

I nodded. "I'm sorry. Really I am. It's just that... well just that I've been sitting around worrying and getting more and more scared for the last half-hour. I guess you got blasted by the first volley."

48

"Scared?"

"Yeah. Right now things are okay. But what if stories get back to Dad or to the studio? What then?"

"My god. You mean you're actually frightened that Brian *might* tell someone that you *may* be gay?"

I nodded again.

"Talk about a closet mentality! Why are you so scared of that?"

"Let's face it," I said, "being known as a homosexual in this town doesn't exactly enhance your reputation. You do know what they say about us?"

"Sure. I sometimes get the feeling gays have been blamed for every ill mankind has ever seen, except maybe Legionnaire's disease. But so what? You're still the same person. If someone doesn't care for you that's his problem, not yours."

"You can say that. You don't have anything to lose."

He shook his head slowly.

"I'm willing to accept your apology. I can chalk the yelling up to a bad case of nerves. However, if you really believe your last statement then this conversation's gotten so asinine that I'm not going to bother sticking around to hear how it comes out."

"And just what's that supposed to mean?"

"Just what I said," he snarled. "Even sunny California's not exactly heaven you know. But I refuse — refuse, damn it — to let a twerp like Brian upset me. My self-respect is important too. I actually happen to like myself. And no one, not Brian, not my folks, not even you is going to take that away from me."

I stared open-mouthed at him. He continued a little more calmly.

"Look, Neil. I didn't wake up one morning yelling, 'Oh, goody. I'm gay.' Don't forget I grew up in your everyday straight family too. I was fed all the usual garbage

49

about gays when I was growing up. Then I found out that's exactly what it was, garbage. You know, my dad still thinks every gay guy wears a dress and high heels." He smiled slightly. "Actually, I look horrid in a dress. Now a slacks outfit and chiffon scarf on the other hand...."

I started to laugh.

"See? The world doesn't stop if you laugh."

"I'm still scared."

He nodded. "Me too. A bit. But let's not worry about something that may not happen."

"Want to go to the beach?" I asked.

"The beach? And you tell me I have a weird sense of logic. How did the beach slip into this conversation?"

"I'm just nervous and I want to do something. We can head for Laguna. It's not much further than Newport and there's a lot of gay people there."

"But it's almost two o'clock."

"It doesn't get dark til seven. We can be there by three. Besides, I can crate up a few of the birds and take them along for a training toss."

"What about your dad? Doesn't he need a ride home from work?"

"I'll call and see if he can catch a ride with one of the guys there."

"If it's fine with him, then I'm game."

Twenty minutes later we were on the road.

10

The traffic was heavy but moving at its usual ten miles per hour over the speed limit. Usual, that is, except when a CHP officer darted out into the stream of traffic like an otter after a fish. We pulled off the freeway during one such flurry of brakelights about thirty miles from the house and I released the pigeons.

"You know, Paul," I said when we were back on the road. "I really am sorry about blowing up at you."

"I'm just glad you came after me. I hadn't planned on ever coming back. I didn't want to cause you any trouble."

I gawked at him.

"You mean, go for good?" For some reason the idea made my stomach queasy.

He nodded. "Uh, Neil. Watch the road, will you please."

"Oh, sure. Damn. I'm sorry, I didn't mean to come on that heavy."

"I know." He squeezed my hand. I relaxed but I couldn't get over the idea of him leaving. I didn't like that thought at all.

We pulled into Laguna Beach and as usual it was packed.

"I've heard all those Beach Boy songs about California surfers," Paul said as we cruised up and down looking for a parking spot, "but I never thought I'd get to see any."

"What do you mean get to see," I said indignantly, "You already have. I used to do some surfing."

"You?"

"Yeah, me. Don't sound so surprised. Actually though I was just a ripple rider. I was happy if the board didn't go flying out from under me when I stood up."

Paul pointed. "There's a VW pulling out."

"Welcome to Laguna," I said as I pulled into the spot, "land of sunshine, sand, and some of the foxiest guys on earth."

"I'll look," he said. "But I already have the foxiest guy."

That floored me. I never thought of myself as foxy. I didn't know what to say. I stared at him. He smiled and touched my hand gently. I knew then.

"I love you, Paul," I said. He smiled again.

"I've been hoping to hear you say that. I fell in love with you the week after I met you."

"Me?"

"Yeah, you. It may have escaped your attention but you're a hell of a lovable person."

That did it. If there were any bigoted straights watching then, they can get over it. I've seen enough of those breeders in heat nearly screwing on the sidewalk along the beach. I grabbed him and kissed him. And no, it wasn't one of those soft gentle romantic kisses. It was hard, passionate, and breathless. I wanted to get all of him into me at that moment. We must have stayed locked together for a few minutes.

"Whew," he said as we came up for air. "Would you rather go fox hunting, or should we rent a room and make out all day? Personally, I'm for the room."

I gave it serious thought for a moment.

"Let's hit the sand," I finally said. "I wouldn't want to be the one who deprived you of the chance to see if the Beach Boys were lying or not."

"Me and my big mouth."

As we were grabbing the towels out of the trunk, he asked me, "Nance wants me to ask you if you know where she could get a Dalmation. Dad said we could finally have a dog now that we're not just renting a place."

"Not really. But if I see anything I'll let her know."

The rest of the afternoon is a blur of great looking guys, some gorgeous women — we looked even if we didn't want to touch — and lots of sun, sand, and meaningless conversation. Meaningless, that is, to anyone else if they had been listening.

On the drive home, Paul kept his head in my lap. I blessed whoever it was who'd invented sunscreen products. If they hadn't I'd have been burned so bad no one could touch me. Yet here I was with a great looking guy lying there, looking at me, and running his finger along my chin.

"You know your nose looks like half a mushroom from this angle?" he said.

"What?"

"I said—"

"I heard you. I just think you're slightly insane."

"Never said I wasn't. In fact, I plan to get my master's in insanity. I figure it's a great preparation for a life in public service."

"Can I ask you something, Paul?"

"Sure."

"How come you told Nancy you're gay and you

didn't tell Jeff? I can see you not telling your folks, but why not him?''

"Jeff and I get along pretty well, but we never seem to talk about anything of importance. It's funny and a little sad really. We used to protect each other in grade school, you know the usual fights, but we seem to have grown differently. We play weird jokes on each other, and I guess I love him, but he's not the kind of guy I'd pick as a friend.''

"What do you mean?''

"He's kind of one way. You loan him something and he never repays the favor. Why do you ask?''

"I've been wondering if I should say anything to Phil.''

"I don't know him that well. I can't tell you. But if he loves you, why not? You're the same guy he's always known.''

"I guess I'll have to give it a lot more thought,'' I said as I pulled around the corner near the house. Paul sat up.

"Good lord! Drive around the corner again. Don't stop,'' Paul said quickly.

"Huh?''

"Just do it. That's my dad's car in your driveway.''

"Your dad? What's he doing here?''

"I don't know. He's never really asked to meet your family, you know.''

"You don't think. . . .'' I asked, suddenly worried.

"I'm not sure. But I have this feeling like there's going to be an earthquake, and I don't like it.''

"Maybe he only stopped by for a cup of coffee?''

"Maybe. But if you really believe that, I have a bridge in Brooklyn I'll sell you *real* cheap.''

"Well, we can't drive around the block all night.''

"I know,'' he sighed. Then he looked at me. ''No

matter what, whether it's a false alarm or not, just remember I love you.''

"Same here," I replied. Paul looked scared. Almost as scared as I felt.

He forced a smile. "Of course, if it's what we think it is, we can't lose.''

"Oh, no.''

"They say love conquers all. Look at Romeo and Juliet.''

"They wound up dead, remember?'' I said dryly.

"Sure. But they achieved immortality.''

"I am right. You are insane.''

I pulled into the driveway on the third pass.

"Hang in there," Paul said as we climbed out. "With any luck they'll be sitting around the TV discussing ball scores.''

They weren't.

11

Paul's dad was sitting at the table next to Mrs. Carrington. Mine was pacing back and forth trying to wear a trench in front of the refrigerator. They didn't even say hello when they saw us.

"They're home," Paul's mom said as she looked up.

"Sit down, boys," Mr. Carrington said. "There's something we'd like to talk to you about."

"What's up, Dad?" Sweat ran down my side as I asked.

"Just sit, Neil. We'll explain everything in a minute."

I sat down next to Paul. He kicked me lightly under the table but I pretended not to notice.

Mrs. Carrington slid two envelopes across the table to us. One was addressed Carrington, the other Meislich. That's all. There was no street address, and no stamp.

"Read them," my dad said.

I pulled out the Meislich letter.

"Your son Neil is a fag. Ask the fruit, Paul." That was all it said. Paul handed me his letter. Only the names were reversed.

"Ordinarily, none of us pays any attention to an unsigned letter," Mrs. Carrington said, "but when your dad called us, Neil, we decided it might be best to let you boys know what was going on."

I was sweating. Paul looked fairly calm but I could see the envelope trembling slightly in his hand. He tossed it casually on the table.

"So?" he said quietly.

"So?" his dad said as he stood. "So. Is it true? Are you queer?"

Paul glared at him. "No!" he said firmly.

I nearly slumped out of my chair in relief.

"I'm gay," he said.

I nearly choked.

"But before you go screaming," Paul continued looking directly at me, "Neil's not."

"Thank god," I heard my father say. It was like a dream.

Everything was happening too fast. Paul's mom just sat there looking stunned. His dad started screaming.

"I knew it. I told you, Janet. He should have been dating three years ago, but no. You kept saying he was just shy. Shy, hell! My own son's a frigging faggot."

Paul turned pale.

"What did we do wrong?" his mom asked sobbing. "Tell me, Paul. What did we do wrong?"

"You didn't do anything wrong, Mom," Paul started to say. "Jeff's not gay and he—"

"You made a pass at your own brother, you disgusting pervert!" His dad screamed as he backhanded Paul so hard he fell halfway out of his chair.

His mom and I were on our feet before the sound of the slap had faded.

"Dave! Stop it!" his mom yelled.

"Touch him again, you bastard," I heard myself yelling, "and I'll put you through the kitchen window in pieces so small they won't be able to find them."

The room seemed to close in. Only Paul and his dad existed for me. I was an observer watching myself help Paul up, but I never took my eyes from his dad. Mr. Carrington looked at me, then backed up.

"You okay?" I asked Paul. He nodded slightly and the room came back into focus.

"Oh, Neil. No!" I heard my dad whisper. I looked around and he was crying. My dad was crying. He knew.

"Paul was only lying to protect me," I said. "I'm just sorry you had to find out like this. I wanted to find my own way to tell you."

Paul slipped his hand into mine and squeezed gently. The left side of his face still showed the imprint of his dad's hand. He pulled away quickly when he saw the looks on our parents' faces.

"When everyone's rational," he said looking pointedly at his father, "we can talk this out. Right now I'm leaving."

He turned, then looked back over his shoulder.

"By the way, Dad. Despite your stupid insinuation, I know Jeff's straight because I have to buy the rubbers he's too embarrassed to get."

"Don't bother coming back," his father said viciously. "Just get your clothes out of the house and keep going."

"David!" his mother screamed.

"Don't you 'David' me, Janet. I am not having a faggot under my roof."

I thought Paul was going to faint.

"He's our son," Mrs. Carrington said.

"Not any more. I want him out."

"Now you listen to me David Carrington." She smashed her palm onto the table. "I don't like this any more than you do. But you are not, I repeat, not, throwing our son into the street. I mean that. Because if Paul goes, so do I, and Nancy, and Jeff.''

Mr. Carrington looked from her to Paul. With obvious effort he said, ''You can stay. But as far as I'm concerned you don't live there. I won't see you. I won't hear you. I have only one son and a daughter. Is that clear?''

Paul nodded numbly. I wanted to cry. Paul walked slowly from the kitchen with his head down. I turned to follow him.

''Neil,'' my dad called. I turned back. ''We have to talk.''

''I know, Dad. But can it wait a bit?''

He started to protest, then looked from Paul's dad to me. He nodded his head wearily. That's when I knew for sure my dad really did love me.

12

Paul was sitting on the corner and just staring up toward the mountains when I found him. I had to step in front of him before he knew I was there. He smiled wanely as I sat down beside him.

"One of my friends in Illinois told his folks," he said almost to himself, "and they all went out for coffee afterwards. Me, I get disinherited."

"Maybe your dad will calm down by the time we get back."

"My dad!" He looked at me as if I were wacky. "No way. If blood feuds were still in style, he'd be in heaven."

"Maybe we could get an apartment."

He smiled. A real smile this time.

"Thank you," he said. "I noticed the *we*. But you can't afford it now that you're out of work, and neither can I." He sighed. "I'll have to play it his way for a while at least. I have this horrible feeling though that it's going to be utter and irrevocable hell."

"I wish I knew something to say that would help you feel better."

"You said it all when you stood between me and

him. My god. I've never seen anyone move so fast in my life. I think you were there before I hit the floor.''

I shrugged. ''Blame it on adrenalin.''

He stared at me a moment then asked softly.

''Would you have really hit him?''

''Yes,'' I said flatly. ''I'm only thankful he didn't try anything else. Right then I might have done more than just hit him.''

''I can't believe he went that berserk. He went off like a bomb.'' He rubbed his cheek. ''You know, I actually like my folks. Yesterday they liked me. Today I'm a fag. Not a son. Not the person they raised. Not even the guy who mowed the lawn yesterday.'' He started to cry, not sobs, just tears running down his face. ''To them I'm a fag, just a goddamn fag.''

''Stop it!'' I snapped. ''I thought you liked yourself. Aren't you the one who sat there and told me that no one, not even your family, was going to take away your self respect? Aren't you the one who said if someone doesn't like you that's his problem, not yours?''

''Sure. But my own dad—''

''I know it's hard. . . .'' I said.

'My god,'' he said sadly. ''I've been so busy feeling sorry for myself I forgot you. What are you going to do?''

I shook my head. ''I haven't had time to wonder yet. Everything's been moving so fast, I've only been reacting to it. I guess I'll talk to my dad but I don't know what I'm going to say. Everything I was planning to tell him seems so pointless now. I was going to lead up to it gradually, and maybe even talk to Phil before I spoke to him.''

''Would it help if I came with you?''

I thought that over. ''No. This has to be between me and him.''

He nodded, then stood up. He looked suddenly much younger in the glare of the streetlight.

"I'm going to walk around the block a few times. I don't have the stomach to go home right now," he said.

"Want some company?"

"No. I've got some thinking to do. Besides, your dad's probably going crazy waiting for you."

"Why do you think I'm still sitting here? I put on a brave act but I'm scared to go home myself." I paused, then asked, "By the way, you're not planning to pull a Romeo on me and do yourself in, are you?"

He reached down and grabbed my shoulder. "Thank you for worrying," he said. "But you're a jerk, you know it? I'm gay, not crazy." He pulled me up and we stood facing each other. Then he hugged me so hard I thought my ribs would break.

"Also, I've got a lot to live for. I love you."

I kissed him lightly on the nose.

"I happen to love you too."

He squeezed me again then pulled away. "You'd better be getting back. I don't want you getting into any more trouble than we have now."

I nodded and he turned to go.

"Paul."

He turned back.

"If it gets absolutely unbearable, give me a call. There are some campsites not too far from here. We can spend a few days there until we figure out what to do."

"Okay. If it comes to that, I will."

I watched him till he turned the far corner, then I headed home.

13

Dad was staring at a cup of cold coffee when I walked back in and sat at the table. He didn't even look up. He just asked quietly, "Would it have made any difference if I'd remarried after your mom died? I thought of it you know. For the sake of you kids. I figured you needed a mother. But I loved her so much. I couldn't bring myself to look at anyone else for three years after she died. Since then, well, I haven't met anyone I want to share my life with."

"Dad," I said softly, "Dad. Look at me please."

He looked up. His eyes were red and puffy.

"I could tell you I know everything about it — but I don't. I'm still finding out myself, but I do know it's nothing you did. It's nothing I did either. It's nothing anyone did. In fact, there's nothing to blame.

"I'm gay, Dad. I guess I've always been though I didn't want to admit it. At least not till I met Paul. He's the best thing that's ever happened to me."

"But what kind of a life will you lead? You're going to wind up with no friends, except maybe some guy in a dress. Maybe it's just a phase. I've heard a lot of guys experiment, then settle down and get married."

"Damn it, Dad. It's not an experiment and I resent you trying to put it on that level. It's like...." I struggled to find the right words. "I don't know, it's like when I met Paul everything I'd been searching for my whole life about myself suddenly jelled. For the first time, I know who I am. And I can tell you I'm not going to wind up friendless. At least I don't think so. I mean, I'm a pretty nice person. I do take after you and Mom, you know."

He smiled. "You also have her habit of trying to stack arguments for your side. Still," he pulled out the letter from his pocket, "what about this? Do you know who wrote it?"

"I've got a good hunch. I think it was Brian."

"That probably means everyone in town will get a verbal report. And school starts Monday. What about that?"

All at once I didn't feel so good. My skin was clammy. I wondered what it was going to be like at school.

"I don't know," I said honestly. "The only ones I was worried about were you and Paul."

"I appreciate that," he said, "but you'd better realize what you're doing." His voice got stronger. "I don't like this. I don't like any part of this, but you're seventeen years old. In a month you'll be legally entitled to do what you want with your life but even more than that I gave up the idea a long time ago that I could ever beat any of my children into something. I've also done my damndest to raise you to be your own man."

"I know, Dad."

"Let me finish. I don't understand you. I thought I did and now I find myself looking at a stranger. I've got to find out about him before I make any decisions. But I love you, Neil. I always have and I always will. I don't say it often because I find it hard to express myself that way, but I do love you."

My eyes were getting a little red and puffy too.

His lips curled in a half smile. "I was actually a little proud of the way you stood up to Paul's dad. He took off from here screaming like a banshee about two minutes after you left. I feel sorry for Paul."

"He's hurting bad. I told him we could camp out for a while if things got too rough at home."

I saw Dad flinch slightly at the idea of us together but he didn't say anything. He just looked up as we heard Phil's car pull in.

"What about Phil? He has to be told," Dad said.

"I know." Suddenly I smashed my hand down on the table. Dad's coffee went flying but we both ignored it.

"What . . . ?" Dad started.

"Damn it. It's not fair," I said furiously. "I wanted to do this in my own way. I wanted you and Phil to know because I love you, not because some turd forces me into telling you." I looked at him. "I've been going crazy for the last few weeks trying to figure out the best way to tell you, and now that's been taken away from me."

Phil walked in and tossed his keys on the table.

"You two look pretty lousy," he said cheerfully. "You also have coffee on the floor."

"Sit down, Phil. We have to talk," Dad said.

"Okay, but can we make it fast? I promised Barbara I'd pick her up so we could go to the movies tonight. After all she's been after me for months and the least I can do is be on time for her to catch me."

He spun a chair around and sat with the back facing forward.

"So, what's up?"

Dad looked at me. I took a deep breath.

"You're liable to hear some rumors that I'm a homosexual."

Phil sat bolt upright.

"Anyone says anything like that to my face, he'll be eating his teeth."

"Phil," I said quietly, "I *am* gay. I'm in love with Paul."

He started to laugh. I expected a lot of things but not that. Then he stopped laughing as he stared at me and Dad.

"You're serious, aren't you?"

I nodded.

"You're a faggot!"

My stomach dropped to my shoes. I knew now how Paul had felt at the taco stand.

"Phil!" Dad yelled.

"That's okay, Dad," I finally said, "The word's gay, Phil. Not faggot. Not queer, not even fruit or pansy. Gay."

"What do you think about this?" he asked Dad, who just shook his head.

"But you don't look quee— I mean gay," he said.

Suddenly I was tired of being reasonable.

"What do you want?" I snapped, "rouge and a dress? I've never worn them and I never will. But I'm still gay and you're going to have to get used to the fact."

"Like hell I do," he snarled as he stood and grabbed his keys. "I'm going to Barbara's." He stormed out.

"*That* was pretty stupid on your part," Dad said.

"Why? Because I'm sick and tired of being gawked at like I'm a new virus? Well, I've had it. Up to my eyebrows, I've had it. This started out to be such a nice day and now...." I pushed my chair back so hard I had to grab it to keep it from going over.

"I'm going to feed the birds," I said disgustedly, "at least, they'll believe I'm the same person I was yesterday."

I flipped on the lights in the loft and sat and watched. One of the youngsters we'd released earlier was missing.

I'd hoped he'd show up in the morning but to be gone after a mere thirty mile toss was a bad sign. Normally, it only takes about forty-five minutes to travel that far. I hoped he hadn't flown into a telephone line somewhere. He was out of good stuff. His mom won the six hundred mile race by over twenty minutes and his dad was always in the top ten percent.

Bombs Away flew onto my shoulder and I gave her a few grains of safflower. The trust she showed was a balm, but then the birds had always been good to me. They had helped me get through my Mom's death.

I whistled the birds down and fed them. Half my mind was worried about everything that was going on, but it was submerged by the calm I felt watching the homers. I can't really explain it but racers mean more to me than any cat or dog we've ever owned. In fact, the one year I went away to summer camp I found myself spending hours at a nearby feedlot just so I could watch some pigeons, even if they were commies.

I'm not sure how long I stayed in the loft. I waited till everyone had taken a second drink and went back to perch again. Then I closed up for the night.

Dad was watching TV when I walked in. He looked up but didn't say anything.

"You were right," I said abruptly. "It was a stupid thing to do. I'm also sorry I blew up at you."

He nodded. "Understood. Today hasn't been the most normal of all days."

"You can say that again," I said fervently.

"I would also suggest you might want to apologize to Phil."

I nodded wearily. "I've already decided to."

He went back to his program and I trudged into the room and lay on the bed. I stared at the ceiling while I waited for Phil and tried to sort everything out. I wanted to call Paul to see how he was getting on, but I didn't dare. I might get his dad.

Phil walked in. I'd been so absorbed worrying I hadn't even heard his car.

'Look . . .'' we both said simultaneously.

"You go first," I said as I sat up. "I owe you that."

He sat on his bed facing me.

"I've been thinking about this all night," he said. "And about a lot of other stuff too. Like how you taught me to tie a fly when we went fishing, and how you kept that guy from beating me up when I was eight."

I smiled. "I remember that. I thought he was going to kill me. He was so old, he must have been what — twelve, thirteen?"

"Yeah," he said gnawing on his knuckle. "And I also remembered all the times we fought and tried to kill each other. Anyway, what I'm saying is that you're my brother. Whatever you want to do with your life I'll stick with you. Now what did you want to say?"

I couldn't talk for a minute. I was too busy trying to stifle tears.

"Only that I wanted to apologize for snapping at you. I had no right. I've had my whole life to get used to the idea, you had forty seconds. On top of that, I also think you're probably the best brother anyone's ever had."

We sat there staring at each other. Neither of us seemed to want to break the spell. Then he coughed and stood up.

"I got to grab a shower," he said.

I watched him rummaging through his dresser drawers.

"Phil," I said as he started to leave.

"Yeah?"

68

"Thank you. You have no idea how much I needed to hear that tonight."

He flipped me a thumb's up.

I curled up and was asleep when he got back.

14

I didn't see much of Paul for the next few days. He called once to let me know he was okay but that Nancy had suggested it might be better if we didn't get together for a while. She thought maybe his dad would cool off.

I'd already tried to call once but his dad answered. He swore at me and hung up, so I figured maybe Nancy was right.

Friday afternoon, Paul stopped by.

"I can't take it anymore," was the first thing he said after he kissed me. "My dad's driving me off the deep end. If you're free, would you like to go someplace, anyplace? I don't care. I just have to get away for a while."

"I know a neat little canyon off the road heading up to Mt. Baldy. We can be there in fifteen minutes."

"Great. Let's go."

I threw together some tuna sandwiches, grabbed my backpack, and we piled into the car.

We didn't speak all the way up, just sat holding hands. Paul watched as the city fell away behind us.

I pulled into a dirt turnout and we hiked down into

the canyon. I gave him the ten cent tour, pointing out the change from coastal sage scrub to riparian woodlands, as we wandered back toward a small waterfall I knew.

Paul was thrilled, especially when I showed him a mass of thousands of hibernating lady bugs in a hollow tree. He'd never been in the mountains before.

We watched a dipper bobbing in and out of the little pond at the base of the falls. From where we were we could see her splash into the water, then walk along the bottom as she used her wings to steady herself. When we got tired, we stretched out on a carpet of needles under a sugar pine and had the sandwiches.

"I feel like a ghost at the house," Paul said after we'd eaten. "If I don't move, Dad barges right into me. I try to eat out whenever I can cause if I'm at the table with him, it's absolute hell. A leper would get more recognition than I do. Thank god for Nancy and Jeff, they're the only things keeping me sane."

"Once when I called for you, he told me he'd never heard of a Paul Carrington," I said as I snuggled up beside him. "Then he swore at me."

Paul shook his head.

"I was talking to my mom last night about getting a job and moving out. I figured that might be the best thing to do. She threw a fit. She said if I didn't finish school, *she'd* never talk to me. I can't win." He looked glum. "How's it going at your place?"

"Better than you have it but I still feel like I'm walking on eggshells. I've been afraid to say too much. I've even stopped asking any of the guys to stop by. Dad and Phil don't say anything, but there's a look in their eyes, like is *this* a new one." I chomped on a piece of grass, and laid back beside him to watch the cloud patterns through the tree branches. I'd almost forgotten how nice he felt, but I remembered quickly with his lap as my pillow.

"They're trying hard to understand but it's difficult for them."

"You know," he said, brushing his finger over my forehead, then down the bridge of my nose. "I'm actually looking forward to school Monday. Anything for an excuse to get out of the house."

"It's liable to be just as bad there."

"It can't possibly be. Even if people throw things at me, at least they'll acknowledge I'm alive. That's more than my dad does."

"If anyone says anything to me, I'll put his teeth down his throat," I vowed.

"Yeah, but then you're the heavy. Sometimes it's better to make them look like jerks if you can." He rolled over onto his stomach and looked at me.

"Like last year. I was walking around a shopping center with one of the guys I knew. We were talking about politics. Anyway, some guy who'd seen my friend do a talk somewhere came up behind us and started to scream, 'You faggot! You lousy faggot!' I didn't know what to do. Everyone was staring. But without a pause, my friend turned around and in the same tone of voice said, 'Look, Harold. Just because *you* couldn't come last night is no reason to let everyone know our business.'

"The idiot looked so small he could have crawled under an earthworm and hid."

I smiled and ran my forefinger along the inside of his thigh.

"God you're handsome," I said.

"We were talking about problems."

"I know. But we can't do anything about them right now, can we?"

He shook his head.

"Then let's forget them. Please. I'm so sick of all that crap. Do you realize we haven't had any time for ourselves since this whole mess started?''

"You're right. And I've missed it.'' He rolled over onto his back and scrunched beside me. I flopped onto my stomach and brushed my lips against his.

"I haven't told you lately,'' he said. "I love you.''

"Um huh.'' I mumbled. "If it's only half of what I feel for you, it's more than enough.''

He pulled me on top of him.

"We have to stop meeting like this,'' I joked.

"Why?''

I tried to roll off and think up an answer but he grabbed me and we started to wrestle playfully.

"Can't think of an answer, can you?'' he asked cheerfully while he tickled my side.

"No,'' I giggled. "No.''

"Good. Then be quiet and come here.'' He pulled me to him again. We kissed. It was a replay of that night we went Green Mist hunting, only this time it was even more fun.

15

Monday morning I met Paul in front of his house about seven a.m.

"Ready to go see if it's going to be a good year or if we should find us a lover's leap," he greeted me cheerfully.

"I'm not keen on heading up to school this morning," I told him.

"That makes it unanimous. But there's no choice. We can't spend our whole lives ditching."

"Why not? We could head into the mountains. Live off the land and become the antithesis of modern man, the heroes of the back-to-the-earth movement."

He smiled. "And you've got the balls to say I'm insane? Besides, if we did do that, who'd feed your birds?"

I shrugged. "Hadn't thought about that."

"Right," he said dryly. "Let's get our asses up to campus and get this over with."

We separated when we hit the school and I didn't see him until lunch.

"How's it been going with you?" he asked as he pulled up a chair beside me in the cafeteria.

"Fine. Not a peep from anyone. Maybe Brian decided wrecking our home life was enough."

"I hope you're right. Here, have a piece of my . . . oh, oh." He nodded toward the door. "I think we relaxed too soon."

I turned and gagged on my sandwich. Brian and three other seniors were heading our way. Everyone was staring at them. Why not? They were prancing and skipping single file. All of them were swishing their hips so hard it's amazing they didn't dislocate them, and each carried a little basket in one hand with the other hand on the shoulder of the guy in front.

They sashayed up to us tossing metallic glitter in all directions and loudly humming the Sugar Plum Fairy.

"Relax, fellas," Brian said to the others as they stopped in front of us. He spoke with a fake lisp and loudly enough to be heard throughout the room.

"I just stopped by to let bygones be bygones," he said to us, "and to apologize for writing those nasty vicious notes to your folks. I was just too, too rotten." He bent his wrist and wiped a fake tear from his eye. The other three were snickering.

Paul and I sat there with our mouths open. There wasn't another sound to be heard in the room. Even the food servers were watching as Brian continued.

"In fact, I was so crushed by my thoughtless callousness I talked to a few of the fellows. You know, like in 'say fellows.' Anyway we thought we'd make up for it by trying our best to make you feel at home." He squealed delightedly. "We know how hard it must be for you to find fairies — after all, most of them spend all day just flitting from pansy to pansy. And you two are definitely the fairiest of the fairies, so here, have some fairy dust."

The four of them threw enough glitter at us to sink a small ocean liner. Paul's curt headshake is all that kept me from throwing my silverware at Brian, then ripping his throat out. Paul forced a smile and brushed the glitter out of his face.

"That is exceedingly thoughtful of you guys," he said jovially and just as loudly as Brian. "Going through all this trouble and just for us."

"It was nothing," Brian said snidely.

"No really," Paul said. "Here we were eating our lunch, minding our own business, and worried that consideration was dead in America. And you guys take the time to swish in, twitter all over the cafeteria, and in general act like four of the biggest stupidest jackasses any human being has ever seen. All for our enjoyment too. That's outstandingly generous of you. Almost as generous as your standing on that side so we don't have to smell you."

There was a buzz of amusement through the room. Brian and his cohorts didn't seem to share it. Ragged shouts of "Queer boy sure has a big mouth" and "Right on, dude," mingled throughout the room.

"Look you fag—" one started to say as I stood up.

"I'd be very careful of what I said from now on if I were you, asshole," I said with a cold smile. Paul grabbed my sleeve but subsided when I shook him off. If I had to fight, I would.

The four of them looked at each other, then back at me. I could see them measuring me, debating silently if they could take me.

Just then Juan walked up carrying his tray.

"Hi, Neil." He sat down facing the four. He nodded to Brian, who had suddenly started whispering to his cohorts, and then he pointedly ignored them. I noticed he placed his tray an inch over the edge of the table so he could grab and use it in a split second. "How are the birds?"

I could have hugged him. Brian and the others faded away. I saw them sit with a few other people at one of the far tables. The room went back to normal, or as normal as could be expected. The hair on the back of my neck was still up and I felt my fist clench spasmodically every time an extra loud "pansy" or "faggot" floated in our direction. I tried hard to concentrate on Paul and Juan but all I wanted was to go stuff some faces in their soup.

"Thanks, Juan," I said as I sat down again and dumped the glitter off my plate. Paul echoed my sentiments. Juan shrugged.

"What are friends for?" he asked. "Besides, I haven't had a chance to get to the studio for three days. I was hoping I could get a workout here."

"Aren't you afraid people will brand you with us?" Paul asked.

"Who cares? I know who I am. Besides, Neil and I go back a long way."

"But why?"

"Look, Neil. I don't care what you two do in bed. I think you're a nice guy. Personally, I happen to like the ladies but that's neither here nor there.

"I thought there was something fishy the day you wanted to show off for Paul at the studio. You were the one who always told me you hated anyone who flaunted the art, but it was none of my business." He looked around the room. It was obvious people were staring. He waved. Two seconds later we dodged an incoming bread roll. Unfortunately none of us saw where it came from.

"You do realize, it's going to be hard for you guys," he said. "Everyone in the school knows. The mouth has been at it all morning. Word was out not to miss lunch; that's why I showed up."

We nodded glumly.

"And Neil," he said in mock seriousness, "I know I'm a wildly attractive man. My mother's told me so. Therefore, would you please try and contain your passionate impulses around me."

Paul burst out laughing. So did I.

"You moron," I said between gasps. "What would I want with something like you when I've got someone like Paul. That's like comparing artichokes to roses."

"I'm crushed," Juan said burying his head in his arms. "Mother was wrong. So wrong. I'm not irresistible." He paused and stood up. "But that's all right. I can live with rejection. I *will* survive. I'll just try to forget my grief in class and if I can't do that I'll get some Twinkies and eat myself into oblivion." He walked off.

"He's a hell of a nice guy," Paul said as he watched Juan leave.

I nodded.

"I expected maybe a little mouthing off," Paul said, "but this?" He looked around the room which was packed with some nasty glances. "I mean, this is California."

I laughed, though my body was still coming off a fighting high.

"Yeah, California. Land of milk and honey, right?" I glanced around the room too. Even the friendlier faces looked away the minute they saw me.

"The bastards," I snarled.

"Believe me, I know how you feel, Neil, but they're not all like that. After all, look at Juan."

"Yeah, but he knows me."

Paul smiled even though I could see he was still upset.

"That's just the point, he *knows* you."

I nodded.

Two black guys walked by. Without saying a word or stopping, one flipped a wad of paper directly on the table in front of us. Paul unrolled it and smiled wryly as he read it.

"We're heroes," he said handing it to me.

"We don't dare come out yet," it read, "but we're with you. Good luck. Raul & Joe. P.S. Loved the touch about jackasses."

I tore it into scraps.

"No need for them to get hassled too," I said as I looked at my watch. "Speaking of hassles we better get to class or we're going to have a few more."

"See you later?" Paul asked after we'd both gotten safely to the exit.

"Yeah. Meet me at the library after your last class and I'll walk home with you."

When I got there Paul greeted me red-faced.

"Remember what I said about I'd rather be at school than home with my dad? Forget it."

We started to walk home.

"What happened?"

"Well, I've been propositioned by two girls who want to take me home and 'cure' me. One even said she didn't find me attractive but she felt obligated to help me.

"I've been handed enough hate literature masquerading as Christian pamphlets to swamp the Enterprise. And I've come very close to stuffing my history book down the throat of that jerk, Brian. He followed me around for fifteen minutes and kept asking me if it's true that fruitcakes cornhole each other. He finally left when one of the girls standing around told him to do something useful, like take a shower. How about you?"

I reached into my pocket and pulled out ten pamphlets. We took turns shredding them as we walked.

"Actually," I said banteringly, "I'm jealous. You always say I'm the foxy one, and *I* didn't have anyone offer to take me home."

"Give the obligated one a few days. She's probably got a backload of cases but I'm sure she'll get to you."

"I don't believe this," I said. "Maybe things will go back to normal once the novelty wears off."

"I hope so. Now I know how movie stars must feel. I can't go anywhere without people pointing and whispering. No, that's a lie," he said. "Dad doesn't point. He just stomps on me. It's gotten so bad I even called that center in L.A. last night. They promised to send me some literature from a group called Parents and Friends of Gays. I thought maybe I could casually scatter it all over the house."

We stopped in front of his house.

"This is rotten you know," he said. "I'm standing here hoping something will keep me from having to walk into that place." He looked at me. "I am so sick of this I don't believe it. Dad seems to think I'm gay only to aggravate him. I stood behind his chair last night and tried to explain there was no choice involved except when I decided to live my life in the light instead of skulking around corners like I was something dirty instead of a person." He shook his head. "I got more response from the chair than I did from him. At least it squeaked occasionally."

"I don't know what to tell you, Paul," I said.

"I know. I'm only using you as a sounding board. Besides, at least you talk back." He sighed.

"I've got to get home and feed the birds."

"Do I get a goodbye hug?"

I looked around.

"Do you really think this is the place?"

He colored a bit, then shrugged.

"Maybe not yet," he said. "I'll see you tomorrow."

"Love you, Paul."

"Love you too."

I was nervous as I walked home. I also felt rotten I hadn't hugged Paul goodbye. Hell, it was only a hug, but I was still worried about what had happened at school. I hadn't told him everything that had gone on; I didn't want to upset him any more than he was. But I'd been threatened by two guys I didn't know. They bragged how they'd mashed the face of a ''fag'' with a beer bottle two weekends before.

They seemed upset that I didn't beg them not to hurt me. They blustered a bit, then split. If they had come a foot closer, I'd have nailed both of them. If I could have been sure they really had beat up some poor guy I would have hit them anyway. But I figured they were just all mouth trying to prove they were bad asses.

I was wrong.

16

Paul called at six-thirty the next morning.

"Can I wait over there while you're getting ready?" he asked. "My dad's being a royal pain."

"Sure. I'll leave the front door open, don't bother knocking. Besides, it's time Dad saw us together again. I don't want him thinking I'm ashamed of you."

I was sprawled under my bed trying to find my other shoe when Paul walked in.

"More problems, Neil," he said. "I just found someone ripped out all the plants that Nance put in. Two guesses why?"

"Shit," I said disgustedly as I stood with my shoe. "What next?"

He shook his head angrily. "I don't know, but I'm getting more than a little fed up with these feeble-brained morons."

I banged on the bathroom door. Phil stuck his soggy head out.

"Cut the pounding for cripes sake," he snapped. "I'll be out in two minutes."

"Make it one. I've got to shave."

"Grow a beard. They're supposed to be making a comeback." He slammed the door and I heard the blow-dryer.

"What did your dad say about the plants?" I asked Paul.

"I didn't stick around to find out. I threw what I could salvage in a bucket of water and left. It's bad enough he kept me up till four-thirty this morning."

"You mean he's talking to you?" I said, astonished.

"Hell, no. Him and mom were just yelling so loud last night I couldn't get to sleep. Now he's claiming *you* corrupted me."

"Me!?"

"Yup." He nodded sagely. "You vicious scheming individual, you. You plucked this innocent child from the straight path, so to speak." He smiled wryly.

I dug a shirt out of the closet. Phil finally sauntered out of the bathroom.

"It's about time," I snarled.

"Cram it." He scooped up his book. "When you're in there it's like waiting for Mary Poppins to get dressed." He turned to Paul. "If it ever works out between you two, don't plan to get into the shower for at least half an hour after him. He uses every drop of hot water in the place."

He got to the door, then turned back. "By the way, tell Dad I won't be home for supper. I'm eating at Barbara's."

I raced for the bathroom and lathered up. "Do you think it's going to be as bad at school today?" I asked Paul.

"Up till the time I saw the plants," he said sitting on the hamper, "I'd have said no. Now I'm not so sure."

"Why don't we... ow!" I said, turning. "go to the beach?"

"You're bleeding."

"Thanks." I stuck some toilet paper on the cut.

"And no," he said. "I told you once I'm not letting any twerp like Brian either ruin, or run, my life. It's getting to the point though where I'd cheerfully go anywhere simply to irritate him."

"In that case, let's go."

We passed Dad in the kitchen, and he nodded to Paul but didn't say anything. I could feel his eyes boring thoughtfully into my back as we grabbed two bananas and left.

Both Paul and I were surprised at school. No one said anything uncalled for all day. It was so calm that after class we sprawled out on the grass and stared up at the mountains which seemed close enough to touch. The Santa Ana winds were blowing near them and the smog was gone.

"Got any plans?" Paul asked as he munched on a pencil.

"Yeah. I've got to stop at the city library to pick up some books on the Byzantines for a history paper, then I'm going over the the studio for a bit. With everything that's gone on, I need a chance to work off some of the aggression I'm developing." I looked at him.

"I've been thinking. The way things are going maybe you should sign up there yourself, or at least let me teach you some basics."

He seemed thoughtful, then said slowly, "I don't like the idea of fighting. At least not for me."

"Neither do I, but unfortunately it's necessary."

"Let me think about it a while. I better be heading home anyway to see about putting those plants back in. Maybe I can do it before Dad gets home. I'll give you a call later on." He started to walk away.

"Paul," I called, "don't you like me anymore?"

He turned back, shocked.

"What would make you say something as stupid as that?"

"You didn't kiss me goodbye," I said teasingly.

"Here?" He looked around, though there wasn't a person to be seen.

I shrugged. "Why not?"

"I thought you were the paranoid one in this duo."

"Me too," I said. "I was worried people might find out I was gay, but who can possibly *not* know by now? And the only people I give a damn about are at home, and here."

He raised an eyebrow. "You're serious, aren't you?"

I sat up and nodded.

He walked back to me smiling and leaned over.

"Welcome to the big wide world beyond the closet door," he said as he gave me a quick peck.

"Love you, Paul," I said squeezing his hand. He smiled again and I watched him leave, then I left myself.

Juan and some of the other black belts were there when I got to the studio. We had a round robin of six attacking one so I put in a hard workout at full speed. By the time I got home it was almost seven and I was exhausted, so I threw a few meat pies and some potatoes in the oven for me and Dad. Then I grabbed some feed and raced for the loft.

I dropped the can as I rounded the corner. What I saw nearly made me puke. Feathers, blood, and mutilated pigeon bodies were everywhere. I spotted Bombs Away near the hedge. Her head had been ripped off. Only one live bird was left — totally spooked by the carnage below. He sat on a telephone pole minus his tail.

I wanted to run, to scream, to hit someone. I was sick to think that anyone could hurt animals like that for no reason. Instead I just cried as I began piling bodies into a heap. My hand trembled as I forced myself to touch

Bombs Away. I still remembered the day she pushed herself from the egg. She'd been so small and defenseless. I remembered her chasing me around begging for food when I had to wean her, and I remembered the day she laid her first egg. She had diplomad that weekend by winning a second overall in the concourse. She had beaten more than two thousand birds from two hundred sixty miles.

I dropped her body on the pile and moved to the loft. It looked like a battlefield, nestboxes ripped from the walls, perches smashed. I also saw the reason for the destruction and death. Scrawled in still drying blood across the front wall was one word: *faggot.*

I went crazy. I ripped the door off its hinges and threw it halfway across the yard. The wall splintered as I kicked it.

"You bastards!" I screamed. "You mindless little bastards."

The incessant ringing of the telephone finally filtered through my rage. I was going to ignore it but then ran into the house hoping it was whoever did it calling to brag. All I needed was a voice, just a voice.

"What the hell do you want?" I snapped as I picked up the receiver. It was Nancy. She was crying. Her answer deflated me immediately.

"Neil. Thank god, I've been trying to get hold of you for hours. You better get down to the hospital. Paul's been hurt. Bad. He's been calling for you."

I don't remember hanging up the phone. I don't remember shutting off the oven or writing a note to Dad and Phil telling them where I'd gone. I don't even remember driving to the hospital. All I do remember is hearing Nancy's voice over and over again. It was like a drum beating inside my head. It reverberated in various combinations. Paul hurt. Hurt bad. Paul calling you.

17

Nancy was sitting in the lobby when I got there. She had stopped crying but she looked so little and vulnerable in the chair.

"What happened?" I asked. "A car accident?"

She shook her head.

"He's sort of incoherent. He just keeps saying over and over again, 'Please don't hurt me anymore. Please don't hurt me.' Then he calls out for you." She looked up at me and began to cry again.

"They beat him so bad, Neil, so bad. He was out looking for a dog for me. I'd called home and he told me he was on the way out with some guy from your studio who knew about a pup for sale."

I knelt down in front of her. She grabbed my shoulders.

"But the worst thing is that whoever it was slashed his face with something. The doctor said probably a razor blade."

"Oh my god," I murmured. "Where is he now?"

"In a room, they've already operated. He was in for almost two hours." Suddenly she gasped. "My god! Are you hurt too? There's dried blood all over your hands, or..." She looked at me with loathing and fear.

"Don't be a damn fool," I said harshly. "The blood's from my birds. Someone killed all of them, but that's not important anymore. I want to see Paul."

"I'm sorry," she said, "I didn't mean to suggest—"

"It's okay. What about Paul?"

"Mom and Jeff are with him now. The office is trying to reach Dad. He's in the field with a late appointment. The doctor said you could see him since he's calling for you."

We took the elevator up in silence. She stopped me as we reached the ward.

"Neil. Try not to look too shocked. They've even taken all the mirrors out of the room so he doesn't accidentally see himself. They're afraid he might lose the will to live."

My heart seemed to stop. We walked in. I nodded abruptly to Mrs. Carrington and Jeff, then almost pushed the nurse out of the way. Only Nancy's warning kept me from going berserk. Paul's face almost didn't exist. His nose was flattened, both eyes were black. Razor cuts had been stitched up on both cheeks and his left ear was bandaged. They told me later that when he came in it had only been hanging on by threads. His whole right side was in a cast and he had so many tubes in him I couldn't believe they'd found enough veins to inject.

"Neil? Is that you?" he whispered hoarsely.

"It's me, Paul," I said taking his hand. "Who did this?"

"I love you, Neil. No matter what, remember I love you."

I started to cry. "I love you too, Paul. More than I've ever loved anything or anyone else in my life."

Suddenly he seemed to withdraw into himself and he

began shaking. His eyes focused on something I couldn't see.

"Please, don't let them hurt me anymore, Neil. Please don't let them hurt me."

"No one will ever hurt you again, no one," I hissed viciously as I brushed the tears from my eyes. "If they come near you, I'll kill them. I swear on my mother's soul, I'll kill them."

Just then Mr. Carrington walked in.

"What in hell is that queer doing here? Get him out!" he said as soon as he saw me.

It was too much. I turned on him. It was like the night in my kitchen, everything was moving in slow motion. Even the nurse left the room at half speed.

"You callous bastard!" I snarled. "Try, you just try to throw me out of here and so help me I *will* break your wrist. The only thing that's stopped me so far is that you're Paul's dad."

His face went scarlet and he started to move on me. As he did he finally saw Paul and he blanched. He was so pale I thought he was going to pass out. Apparently, Jeff did too because he was suddenly standing there propping up his dad's arm.

"You okay, Dad? he asked worriedly.

Mr. Carrington mumbled something.

"What?" Jeff asked.

"Help me outside. Janet, I want to see you." All three disappeared into the hall. Jeff walked back in a minute later, looked at me and Nancy and shrugged.

Paul began begging not to be hurt again. I started to shake and then to cry softly. Jeff walked over and put his arm around my shoulder.

"Stop it," he said softly. "You can't afford the luxury right now. Paul needs us to be stronger than maybe we really are."

"He's right, you know," Nancy said.

I nodded and tried to force the tears back down. I turned back to Paul just as the doctor walked in and threw us all out for upsetting his patient.

Nancy and Jeff stayed with their folks. I walked to the elevator, and was standing there waiting for the car and trying to figure out what to do when I heard Mr. Carrington.

"Neil. I'm sorry. My wife just read me the riot act and as much as I may personally dislike the idea, I think that this time she's right. You can see Paul as often as you like. Anything is okay if it will help him get better."

I turned. He was standing there with his hand out for me to shake. I simply stared at it.

"You've got every reason to despise me," he said, dropping his hand. "Paul has even more, but despite what you think I do love my son."

The elevator doors opened behind me and I looked over my shoulder.

"Go ahead," I said to the lady standing in the car. "I'll catch the next one."

"Love him?" I said softly, viciously. "You sure have a hell of a funny way of showing it. You disown him. You ignore him. You insult him. You seem to spend every waking minute trying to split us up, and you call that love. Thank god my father apparently hates me then. If he loved me the same way you love Paul, I don't think I could stand it. I'm not as brave as Paul is."

I saw him flinch with every word, and heaven help me but I was glad I had hurt him, that I had made him feel a smidgeon of what Paul had gone through.

He looked at me for a minute.

"I guess I had that coming. And more." His voice got a notch stronger. "I just wish I was as sure of everything as you seem to be. It must be nice to be perfect."

"What's that supposed to mean?"

"You're so sure you two are right. Well, I've known a few queer... I mean homosexuals when I was in college. I've never seen more miserable, unhappy, and unloved creatures in my life. One was even a roommate of mine. The son of a bitch had the balls to make a pass at me one night when we were drunk. I finally told him I'd break his arm if he came near me. He was so unhinged he finally killed himself. I found him one morning with a rope around his neck and the gas on just to make sure. I hoped I could keep Paul from that."

I stared at him. At that second I could feel all my hatred of him vanish. All the rancor melted like snow in a blast furnace.

"I feel sorry for you," I said as I punched the call button. "Maybe with that warped thinking you have, you actually thought you were doing the right thing. I don't know. It's people like you who forced your roommate and others like him into living a lie and then hating and despising themselves for doing so. I know that feeling well; Paul helped me get over it. You force them to scurry around trying to hide, to snatch a minute's love and when they do find it you tell them they're sick for wanting it. You use every means possible to break them. If some poor guy does go and kill himself because he's been goaded beyond human endurance, you use that as ammunition against those who won't." I shook my head in disgust. "Of course some are miserable, you and your hatred do your best to keep them that way. Paul is lying in there because of people like you. Think of that, because whether he lives or dies, you're going to have to remember that. Paul and I aren't going to let you or anyone else drive us crazy. You can all go to hell first. We *know* we're worth something as people. Nothing you can say is going to take that away."

The elevator doors opened again. I stepped in and held the door open.

"But go apologize to Paul. It won't make up for the hurt, but it *might* help keep him alive." I let the doors close and stood there as the car dropped. I started to shake.

I was halfway across the lobby, lost in my own misery, when Dad grabbed me.

"Are you okay?" he demanded. From what I could see through my tears he seemed terrified. "You're not hurt?"

"Hurt? Me? No, why?"

He shook me slightly. "You leave a scrawled note that there's been a terrible accident and that you're at the hospital. There are dead birds all over the yard, blood everywhere. Then you ask me, why?"

"Note?"

The ex-sergeant in him came out. "Neil!" he snapped. "What is going on here?"

His voice was a slap across my face. I stopped crying and told him about Paul.

"Were the birds part of that too?"

I nodded.

"I'm glad you weren't home then. They might have tried the same to you."

I went cold all over. I hadn't thought of that. What if they had tried to jump me? Then from deep inside, like a light going on, I realized that I relished the idea. I prayed they would try it. If Paul died I didn't have anything to live for anyway, and I could at least take a few of them with me. A cold smile replaced the tears. I knew I wouldn't be crying again.

Dad looked at me sharply. He spoke so softly I almost didn't hear.

"I've seen that look before in other men's eyes," he said. "A long time ago before you were born, during the war. Usually, just before they did something that left someone dead. Neil, please. Promise me you won't do anything stupid."

I pulled back a few feet. For the first time in my life, I looked at him, not simply as my father but as another man — a man I wasn't sure understood what I was feeling. We stood face to face for thirty seconds, then I said quietly, "Stupid? No, I don't plan to do anything stupid, so I can promise you that. But I will not promise to do nothing."

"Neil, son. Let the police handle it. This is not a war zone. We have laws."

I exploded. "Not a war zone! What do you call it when sadistic bastards mutilate fifty defenseless pigeons? What is it when a group ratpacks a guy whose *only* fault is loving me and then they beat him so badly he may die. Where were the damn police then? Shit, knowing some of the cops in this town they would have stood there and cheered. After all," I said bitterly, "Paul's only a faggot. We all know it's okay to bash a queer. Remember kill a queer for Christ."

I turned and stormed from the lobby, oblivious to the stares.

It was hours before I headed home. The first rage died as I walked around the college campus. It flared briefly when I passed a guy and his girl walking along laughing quietly at some joke. I wanted to smash their faces into the asphalt, to stomp them so hard they'd never move again. How dare they be happy when Paul was lying in the hospital, put there by people like them!

I angled over toward them but then, as if he were lying beside me, I could hear Paul — Paul, who didn't even want me to hit Brian. That's when I went home.

Dad was sitting at the table. He didn't say a word as I

walked by him. I had my hand on the bedroom door, then I turned and went back to the kitchen.

"It seems lately I'm always apologizing to you," I said. "I'm sorry. I shouldn't have blown up like that at you. You had nothing to do with it. It's just, just..." I stopped.

"Nancy called. The doctor told them Paul was probably going to be all right. He's going to need some reconstructive surgery but he'll live."

I sank into a chair and sat there for a minute.

"Why is everyone so scared of us, Dad?" I asked almost in a whisper. "Are we that threatening? We're not plotting the overthrow of the government. We're not doing anything except asking to be let alone. Why would anyone want to hurt Paul so bad?"

He shrugged.

"You're different. That's all the excuse some people need."

"But how different? I sleep. I cry. I eat. I even hate taking math exams. All I do is love Paul. Why is that such a threat to someone else?"

"I don't honestly know. I'm still trying to work some things out in my own mind. That's one of them."

"But Dad? Don't..." I stopped. Suddenly it clicked. Nancy had said something at the hospital that was important but what was it? Damn it, what?

I raced for the phone, knocking the chair backwards as I did so. I heard it fall and Dad's startled squawk but I didn't pay attention to either.

I keyed the numbers so fast I got a dial tone again so I forced myself to relax and punched out Nancy's number one more time. Jeff answered on the twelfth ring.

"Let me talk to Nancy," I yelled.

"Neil?" he grumbled, "It's after one o'clock. She's sleeping. She's pretty shook up about Paul. Can't

94

whatever it is wait until morning?"

"No. She said something at the hospital. I don't remember what, Jeff, but it's urgent. Something about who may have beat Paul up."

"Hang on," he said excitedly.

I heard the receiver banging against the wall as he ran off. I turned to see Dad standing quietly behind me.

"What is it, Neil?" Nancy asked after what seemed an interminable wait, but was probably only thirty seconds.

"Nance. You said something when I first got to the hospital, what was it?"

"I don't remember," she said sleepily.

"Try, Nance. Please! I know it was important but it went right over my head at the time because all I could think about was Paul."

"Let me see. You came in and I said Paul was hurt. That he'd been out looking for a Dalmation pup because someone from the studio—"

"That's it!" I screamed. "Someone from the studio. I never told anyone there about looking for a pup. And as far as I know, no one there knows your address. How did anyone know you were looking for a dog? Did you tell anyone?"

"Not me." Her voice was tense. "I asked Paul to tell you, and I told that jerk Brian when he was over here a few weeks ago. That's it though. With classes starting at the college I've forgotten about it a bit."

"Did you or Jeff see the guy who showed up?"

"No. I wasn't home. Hang on a sec." I heard her mumbling to Jeff. "Jeff wasn't home either. He's checking with the folks." There was another longer pause. "Neither of them knows anything either."

"Thanks, Nance," I said. "I'll take it from here." I hung up and turned to face Dad.

"I got most of it," he said.

"Paul's only been to the studio once," I said, "that first Saturday I met him and... Oh my god!" I almost collapsed on the phone table. "Not Juan." I wanted to bawl.

"Juan?" Dad asked. "Juan Espinosa, the kid who's been coming over for four years?"

I nodded glumly. "I don't see who else."

"I thought you said he helped you at school."

"He did. That's one reason it doesn't make any sense. Another is, he's not the kind of guy to go pounding on someone for no reason. It's just not like him. But who else does Paul know from the studio?"

Dad shrugged.

"What you really need is to get some sleep," he said. "We can't do anything more tonight anyway."

"You're right. In fact, I'm beginning to think you always are."

He laughed. The first honest laugh I'd heard from him since the whole hassle began.

"You know better than that. You're just catching me on a lucky streak." He threw his arm around my shoulder. "Get some sleep, Neil."

"Night, Dad."

Phil woke up when I came in. He propped himself up on one arm and watched me getting undressed. After a minute or so he said, "I'm sorry about Paul."

I nodded.

"I also cleaned up that mess out back," he continued. "I put all the bodies in a trash bag and dumped them in the bin behind the supermarket. I didn't think you'd have the heart to do it." He stopped for a minute then his voice got so harsh I stared aghast. Phil's an easygoing kid. "If you need any help smashing a few faces, I'd love to give you a hand. I haven't forgotten *everything* you showed me.''

"Thanks, Phil. If I do, I'll remember.''

I shut the light and laid down. I heard Phil begin to snore. I finally fell asleep as dawn broke.

18

I slept in late and skipped school, then headed for the hospital as soon as visiting hours started. They wouldn't let me near Paul until I vowed not to ask him anything about the assault. His doctor told me they were planning to have a psychiatrist visit him that evening because he seemed to have blocked all memory of events from an hour or so before his attack until the time he woke up in the hospital. Any questions upset him. When the police had arrived to talk to him earlier, it had taken his nurse two hours to calm him down again. While they didn't anticipate any difficulties they wanted him to get through the block soon so there wouldn't be any chance of lasting psychological trauma. The fact that it was another problem for Paul, though, fueled my anger.

"Hi." He sounded happy to see me walk in.

It was hard to understand him. He looked even worse than before. Everything had swollen and turned purple and black.

"How are you?" I asked.

"Half doped up and floating." He tried to smile but it came out as a grimace. "Do you have any idea what some people would pay for a high like I'm on, and I'd trade it in a second to be in my own bed."

"They'll only let me stay a few minutes," I told him.

He nodded and tried to sit up a hair but because of the plaster and wires he gave that up as a bad idea.

"Tell me honestly," he asked, "how bad do I look? There's not a mirror in sight and I can't get a straight answer from anyone, Doctor, Mom, or Nance. Even my dad won't tell me. Did I tell you he's talking to me again? At least something good came out of this."

I could feel sweat beading on my forehead as I recalled what Nancy had said about the mirrors and there was no one available to ask if he could handle the truth. Then I noticed his eyes peering out from behind all that swollen and mutilated flesh and I played a gut hunch.

"You look as if you've been attacked and mauled by an angry hippo who couldn't wait to wipe you off on the nearest bush."

"Thank you." His voice was quiet. "Even through the drugs that's how I feel. I'm glad to see it's for a good reason." He closed his eyes and I thought he'd fallen asleep so I turned to leave.

"Neil," he said tensely but so quietly I could barely hear him. "Neil, I'm drugged up just enough to tell you something I wouldn't have the guts to do if I weren't. I didn't know how bad I looked but I overheard the doctor talking to my dad when they thought I was asleep. I know I need plastic surgery. If I'm so ugly now that you'd be ashamed to be seen with me you don't have to stick around out of sympathy. I'd never do that to you, you could have anyone you wanted. After all, we never really made any sort of commitment."

"Why you stupid son of—" I started as I walked over to his bed. "Do you actually believe that little piece of maudlin melodrama makes me think you're noble? It

99

simply shows you're not as bright as I've always given you credit for. I'm in love with you, Paul. You. That little person inside that carcass. I don't care if you've got six arms and no legs, or whether your hair is purple with starfish in it. Is that clear?"

He tried to smile. "I was hoping you'd say that," he mumbled. "By the way, Nance told me about your birds. I know what they meant to you."

I felt my throat catch.

A nurse stuck his head in the door. "Time's up," he said to me. "You'll have to leave now."

"Love you, Paul."

"Love you too. And Neil, thanks."

I had my hand on the door but I couldn't leave. I had to know.

"By the way, Juan said to say hi."

"Tell him thanks, and tell him even if his mom does think he's irresistible, if he makes a pass at you while I'm laid up, I'll bite him in the ankle as soon as I can crawl."

I floated to the elevator but came down with a thump when I remembered that since Paul's memory had blanked out, Juan might still be responsible. I decided to find out for sure.

Juan was dribbling a soccer ball on his lawn when I sauntered up.

"I spoke to Phil at lunch," he said as he scooped the ball under his arm. "I'm sorry to hear about Paul. You guys or the police got any ideas who did it?"

"Not yet." I watched his eyes. "But Paul had left a note for Nancy telling her where he'd gone and he mentioned something about someone from the studio. No name or anything but I figure whoever it was lured him out so his friends could clobber him."

For a full fifteen seconds he locked eyes with me, then he heaved the ball straight at my head. I dodged but it caught me in the right ear.

"Why you psychotic bastard!" he snarled. 'You think it was me, don't you? After all these years and you don't know me better than that."

He stormed toward the house yelling back over his shoulder.

"Apparently coming out rotted what passes for your feeble excuse of a brain. I thought we were friends. When have I ever lied to you or done anything to hurt you?" He smashed the door closed so hard, the frame rattled.

To my shame, I stood there debating whether he was for real or simply a consummate actor. Two things decided me: first, even at K-Mart I heard he'd been an outrageous ham; second, and more important, he never had lied to me in all the time I'd known him. I chased after him and followed him into his living room.

"It better be damn good," he snapped, spinning around when he heard the door behind him. "Or one of us is going to get badly hurt when I throw you out."

I could feel myself blushing as I stood there with my head down. "Is an abject apology good enough?" I asked. "I'm sorry. Thinking it might be you has been making me sick, I honestly couldn't believe it, but I had to be sure. I had to be." I sank onto the couch and stuck my head in my hands. "You ought to see him, Juan. I've never seen anyone that mutilated in my life. It's a miracle he wasn't killed. They beat him into unconsciousness, then it looks like they beat him some more. I don't know how he managed to keep all his teeth unless he curled up or they decided slashing off an ear and cutting up his face was enough."

Even without looking up, I could feel Juan staring at me, weighing my words. The silence seemed interminable.

"Apology accepted," he said finally. That was all.

I glanced up. He stood there.

101

"You're not making this easy, are you?" I asked.

He shook his head. "Why should I? I understand part of what you're going through but I'm hurt you'd think I did it." He smiled sadly. "I'll get over it in a bit, but right now I wish you would go home."

I stood and walked slowly to the door.

"I really am sorry."

"Okay, but I'm just as really hurt."

I left and trudged home. As I walked I tried to remember who was working out that Saturday but I couldn't. After so many years, all workouts run together.

Dad screamed for ten minutes when I told him. The gist of it was that I was an overzealous jackass who was trying to play junior policeman and that I'd be lucky if I hadn't irreparably damaged a friendship. He also got in a good half dozen I-told-you-so's. I sat there getting more and more angry, not with him, with me. He was right. When he finally wound down, I went out back to put some feed and water down for the one bird left. He was still perched on the telephone pole and I knew he had been so terrified, he might never come down again. He'd probably wander off to join a flock of commons, assuming a cat or owl didn't snatch him first.

As I glanced around the yard, I seemed to still hear the cooing and see Bombs Away perched on the clothesline upright as she tried to entice me to give her some safflower. I couldn't take it; I had to get away for a while, if only to walk around the block a few times.

19

I spotted Brian and four other guys as I turned the corner. Danny Mello was one of them; that explained what Paul had said. Mello was at the studio that Saturday and he must have stopped by with some fake story about a dalmation. Apparently, Mello knew one of Brian's friends or Brian himself. Two more looked familiar but I couldn't.... suddenly I placed them. They were the two who hassled me at school and bragged about clobbering some poor gay guy. One was still in a baseball uniform and cleats. I noticed he was holding a bat by his side.

I stepped off the curb and started to walk around them. Dad was right. It was a job for the police.

"Hey, faggot!" Brian yelled as they moved to intercept me.

I kept walking.

"Hey, Tinkerbell," Danny yelled. "Don't keep flitting down the street when a man talks to you. Stay put. It saves us the trouble of finding you again."

I stopped. They were in a semi-circle in front and to my left side. My back was safe, at least for the moment.

"Look, you assholes. I've taken all the bullshit from you I'm going to. So bug off."

"Aw! Poor baby." The one with the bat threw his hand on his hip and swished back and forth. "Is the widdle kung-fu creepie angwy with us? I'm so-o-o terrified, I may even faint." He staggered back. "Oh, oh. Catch me. I'm swooning." He fell into the arms of his buddy.

Two moved slightly more to my left. I watched them; they were still out of range.

"Looky," Danny said as he held out a limp-wristed hand. "I'm queer, I'm queer. And I'm so utterly adorable. You want to make it with me, Tinkerbell?"

"No thanks," I said quietly. "I prefer men."

They suddenly seemed to be moving slowly, just like at the house and the hospital. I could feel the adrenalin surge again. Only this time I wasn't mad. I was coldly calculating their positions in relation to me. They could still back off if they chose to.

The others giggled at Danny.

"You going to let a fag talk to you like that?" Brian asked him. "Especially after that pansy Paul tried to knee you in the groin when you grabbed him?"

They moved even slower.

"I'm about to acquaint you five with a truism," I said coldly. "Something I learned in literature from a book by Saroyan. He said, 'Every man in the world is better than someone and not as good as someone else.' Well, assholes, today you've met the somebody who's so much better than you, you're dead."

"Oh, wowie! A literate fag," said the one with the bat as he banged it against the ground.

"You know you've got a big mouth for a pansy," Brian snapped. "Almost as big a one as that fruity friend of yours had till we beat it out of him."

"Remember that smart-ass joke he made when you told him all queers should get out of the U.S. before they were killed?" Danny snickered.

"You mean when he said red, white and blue equals lavender, so that made him an All-American boy? Sure, I remember the commie pervert."

"Yeah," giggled the one standing beside him. "He wasn't so snotty when we finished with him. He barely even squealed when I cut his pretty pansy face." He looked at me. "That was almost as much fun as ripping the heads off those lousy pigeons."

They all roared.

"Yeah," Brian said. "They flopped around real pretty, didn't they?"

I didn't say anything, I just shifted my weight so I could move in any direction necessary.

"What are you smiling about?" Danny snapped.

I didn't even realize I was.

"Think you're good, don't you?" he said. "Well, I've worked with you at the studio. You're not such a hot shit. I've nailed you a few times and you never even came close to hitting me."

That's when Brian and one other rushed me. I dropped them both together — Brian with a right kick to his groin, the other with a palm wipe to the nose. I felt his nose break under my hand. The three who were left stood gaping. Then the jerk with the bat began his attack.

If he'd sent me a letter three days before, he couldn't have given me any more notice. I jammed his arm as he began his swing, and I rammed my right thumb into his eye. He blubbered and I wrenched the bat away as he tried to cover his face. Then I put him down with a vicious sidekick to his ribs.

Danny was already moving on me. I slid under his attack as he snapped a fair roundhouse kick at my head. I blocked it with the bat and heard the crunch as his knee snapped. He landed beside Brian.

Behind me I heard footsteps of the last one running up fast. I rolled away and came up facing him. He seemed stunned to find me looking at him.

"What's the matter, big mouth?" I taunted him. "Is this poor little queer better than all you so-called macho types? Queer-bashing isn't as much fun when it's the queer doing the bashing, is it?"

He dropped into a crouch. I could see he was holding a knife.

"Think you're hot shit, huh fag? Well come on. Come on." He waved the knife around in small circles. His voice trembled, so did his hand.

Out of the corner of my eye, I spied Brian crawling in my direction and struggling to get up. I side-shuffled so I could keep the knife in view and kicked Brian behind the ear. He went to sleep.

"You keep moving away, queer," the one with the knife snarled.

"You so anxious to join your buddies?" I sneered, taunting him by only holding the bat in two fingers.

"I'll make you and that faggy friend of yours a matched set. Only you I'll castrate too so you'll look like the woman you are."

He moved closer, then lunged suddenly as he tried a backhanded slash at my face.

I fell away to the left, flowing with the momentum of his attack, then I moved behind him and locked the bat across his throat as I forced him off balance with my knee, hanging him on the bat. He tried reaching me with the blade but I controlled his shoulder. His struggles were rapidly growing weaker.

"Slash Paul, will you, you bastard!" I hissed in his ear as he began to faint. "Then say hello to the devil when you see him today." I applied more pressure. The blade clattered from his hand.

"Hold it! Now!" The edged words cut through my fury like a buzz saw.

I glanced up to see two cops standing out of range. One had a gun drawn and leveled at me. I looked from them to the guy I was choking. He was turning blue.

"Release him!" the cop snapped.

Reluctantly I let him drop. I allowed the bat to accidentally fall across his face as he did.

Both cops were taking in the scene with incredulous stares. I looked around. Danny was moaning, holding his leg, and puking. Brian was out cold. The guy with the broken nose was sitting on the curb holding his face and crying. Blood streamed from between his fingers. Bat boy was holding his side and face and trying not to wretch. I found out later my kick had broken four of his ribs. The other was still unconscious at my feet. It didn't look good for me at all.

"Move over to the car," one cop yelled. He kept the gun trained on me. "Stand there. Don't move."

I sidled over. The second cop moved to the other side of the car and I heard him radio for an ambulance. Then he was behind me planting my face into the car as he spread my legs and none too gently frisked me. By now the street was full of people.

"Officer. Officer. You've got the wrong one. You should be arresting those ruffians," I heard a woman say. I glanced around from my spread on the car to see a lady who must have been at least seventy-four.

"Who are you, ma'am?" the cop standing over me asked.

"I'm the one who called you. I'm Mrs. Gonzales. I was right there." She pointed across the street. "Right there in my garden watering my mums when it happened.

This young man came around the corner and tried to avoid everything. He even walked out into the street to avoid these hoodlums, but they wouldn't let him.''

I said a silent thank-you to Dad and his advice.

"Then they attacked him. It was marvelous. He knocked two of them down right away. He looked like someone in those karate movies they have on television. That's when I called you. I never believed he wouldn't be badly hurt by them. There were so many and they had that bat.''

One cop looked at me, the other one was keeping the crowds back.

"Black belt. Kung-fu,'' I said to him a hair too smugly.

"We'll need a statement from you.'' He let me stand up.

I nodded. "By the way, they admitted they were the ones who mugged and nearly killed Paul Carrington. You probably have that report.''

He looked interested. "I sure do. I was the one who found the poor kid lying in the gutter. He was a mess. It's going to be a pleasure dealing with these guys.'' He glanced around. "They'll never believe this at the station when I tell them. Normally, we find some poor schnook who's been attacked and nearly beaten to death. They'll love it when I tell them you walked away and they were on the ground. You a friend of Carrington's?''

I thought of Paul in the hospital, I thought of his dad's anger, and the day Brian and the others hassled us at school. I saw the bat and knife on the ground, then looked directly into his eyes.

"I'm his lover,'' I said flatly.

A smile so faint I almost wasn't sure it was there touched his lips.

"I won't mention *that* at the station,'' he said so very

softly I had to strain to hear him. "But I'm glad you found them first. I know how I'd feel if it were my lover."

I gawked at him.

"We *are* everywhere, you know," he said with a hint more of a smile. Then suddenly he was all business again as the ambulance pulled up. I stood to the side until they were loading Danny.

"Mello," I said sarcastically as they gave him a shot for the pain, "I warned you, you were a nothing. You think because I don't like to hurt means I can't. I'm simply so far beyond you and your friends as a fighter, that you're merely bad jokes. Jokes it was a pleasure to erase."

He tried to say something, but threw up again instead. I smiled. The ambulance attendants had the cops drag me away. After they took my statement they let me go home. I walked on air most of the way there.

"I'm sorry," I told Phil when I strode in, "I couldn't take you up on your offer to help me smash a few faces. The five guys who killed all the birds and jumped Paul tried it with me. They're sacked out in the hospital now. Later on they'll be busted."

He made me tell him everything, then spent the rest of the afternoon on the phone calling friends and bragging. I love him.

Dad hit the roof when he came home, right after he found out I wasn't hurt. He cooled down rapidly when I explained that even the cops knew I didn't start it, merely finished something I was forced into. After that, he chased Phil off the phone and started calling *his* friends to brag. There's nothing like family to make you feel loved.

20

The next few weeks dragged by. Word got out naturally, though the flappy mouths at school seemed to clam up — at least when I was around. I tried to keep a low profile and my mind on my classwork but it was hard. So was coming home to an empty yard. I just couldn't handle trying to start a new loft, at least not yet. Two of the guys at the club offered to loan me any breeding stock I needed, one other tried to get me kicked out. I think he was afraid I might try to rape his cock birds or something. I kept up my membership partly to aggravate him and partly in case I decided to fly again.

One afternoon about a month after the attack I was having a sandwich and lounging at a sidewalk table of a local restaurant. The cop who had braced me the day of the fight was cruising by and he pulled over when he saw me.

"Hi," he said smiling as he got out of the car. "Mind if I sit for a moment?"

I glanced up as he came near me. I hadn't noticed how big he was the last time. He must have stood six-feet-four and it was all muscle.

"Have a seat," I said.

I noticed a few looks of distaste from some of the college-type customers as he did so.

"God," I whispered. "They don't like you if you're a cop, or if you're gay. You can't win."

He shrugged indifferently. "I've gotten used to it. Besides, they scream for me fast enough when they need help. How's your lover?"

"Doing real good," I said. "You know, for the last few weeks I'd been hoping to bump into you again. I really wanted to meet you but I didn't know if it would mean trouble for you at the station if I came down there to ask."

"Probably not. Lots of people come in asking for an officer for one reason or another. By the way, my name's Vince."

"Neil."

"I know." He smiled. "Look," he said pulling out pen and paper and scribbling rapidly, "I'm going to do something I almost never do.

"Here's my home number and address. Why don't you call me some night and stop by? I've told my lover all about you and he thought it would be a good idea too. He'd love to meet you. His name's Tony." He slid me the paper. "The only thing I ask is that you please don't go spreading that information all over town. I happen to like my job."

"I don't..." I started. "Hell, thanks, I'd love to. I know Paul will too as soon as they let him out."

"Great. I've got to get going. If you're free why not call tonight or tomorrow? If you get Tony, just tell him I spoke to you today."

I watched him drive off, then I finally got my jaw back where it belonged. I could still barely believe it, a gay cop. I mean, I knew there were but... oh hell, it was like a part of me still bought all that bilge about gay men being only hairdressers.

Next night I called, then stopped by. The two had a nice condo in Diamond Bar. Tony was thirty-three and two years older than Vince. He was about Paul's height but not as skinny and he was Operations Officer at First Interstate Bank.

Within ten minutes we were all sprawled on the living room floor having Pepsis and I felt like they were old friends, though quite honestly I was still in awe of them. I'd never known a gay couple. Even with all my reading I wasn't sure what to expect.

"But what's it like?" I finally asked after an hour of casual conversation. "I mean, how long have you been together? Do you fight? What's it like to be living together?"

Vince threw his stockinged feet up over the back of the sofa and leaned against Tony.

"Fight? Us? Never, not once in the six years we've been together."

"Five," Tony snapped.

"Six," Vince growled.

"Five," Tony snarled as he grabbed Vince loosely around the neck and pretended to shake and strangle him.

I started to laugh.

Vince gulped and grudgingly gave in.

"All right, five." He looked at me as solemn as a basset hound, then both exploded in laughter. Tony mugged.

"No. We never fight. We also never eat, sleep, or want privacy." He paused. "Seriously though, I met Vince exactly five years ago next month at a Whitman-Brooks conference in Los Angeles. I saw him standing near a table. I think I accidentally stepped on three people to get into a position where I could casually meet him." He smiled. "I admit it, it started out as lust at first sight and rapidly moved to love. He rumpled Vince's hair. "He's a hell of a nice guy."

"Ah gosh," Vince drawled looking into Tony's eyes. "You're just saying that 'cause it's true." He pulled Tony down and kissed him.

"Paul's going to love you guys," I said. "You're as crazy as he is."

"When did you say he was getting out of the hospital?" Tony asked.

"When I spoke to him today, he said by next week." Vince looked at Tony.

"Do you think Pat and Laura would mind if they came along?" he asked.

"Not at all. They said to bring a few friends." He smiled. "I think that's what we're all becoming."

"Good. Look, Neil. On the tenth of next month a lesbian couple we know is having a small anniversary party for us. We'd love to have you and Paul there. What do you say?"

I couldn't believe it. A few months ago I didn't know another gay person, and now . . .

"Hell, yes!"

Paul was thrilled the next day when I told him. As for me, I had a thousand questions I wanted answered.

21

Paul was finished with his second trip to the plastic surgeon by the time Brian and his goon squad were yanked into court. Thankfully, they were all over eighteen so they were tried as adults.

It came out those jerks who hassled me at school really had mashed some poor guy's face with a beer bottle. His ''crime'' had been to go dancing and they clobbered him when he left the bar. They had also been responsible for slashing tires and busting windshields out of cars that belonged to anyone who didn't fit their stereotypical idea of a ''real'' man. That definition apparently meant anyone who didn't look, walk, and talk like they did.

It seems they talked Brian and Danny Mello into helping them get Paul, and into trying to get me. At least that was Brian's version. He was doing some glib yammering and claiming he was forced into it against his will. He also denied that he personally had ever disliked any gay person. To hear him talk, he was a brother to the entire gay community. Paul nearly lost his composure over that one but his lawyer dragged him back into his seat and told him to shut up.

They settled by having all Paul's medical bills paid and putting the five on probation for a year. I nearly went berserk myself over that. Attempted murder is what it was, and they got off with probation. Paul calmed me down.

"It's better than what happened in Arizona a few years ago," he said. "I remember reading two college types killed a gay guy outside a bar. They beat him for over ten minutes. The judge let them off because they were good boys who didn't smoke pot."

I still didn't like it but there was nothing I could do.

Naturally Paul missed his senior year, so when I graduated I took a year off school. Dad agreed with my reasons. Not only could I work to put some money away, I also needed a break after twelve years in school. Besides, I could be with Paul and we could enter college together as freshmen.

The surgeons were great. Paul is even better looking, if that's possible, than he was before the assault. One doctor told us that wasn't always the case, but Paul hadn't had any massive skeletal damage to the head. I thanked heavens for that.

In fact, one night not long ago when we double-dated with Juan and his girl, our waitress spent most of the meal cruising Paul and ignoring the rest of us. Poor Juan, that's when he vowed never to believe his mom again.

After much soul-searching Paul and I decided not to go away to school, instead we chose Cal Poly in Pomona. They have a good biology program for me and a good business program for Paul. Yup, he changed his mind again. They've also got an active Gay Student Union.

Paul and I are committed to making it as a couple. We have no illusions, those vanished on the street and in the courtroom, but we think we can make it. At least we stand as much chance as any other couple, straight or gay. We've got Tony's and Vince's advice when we have one of those non-fights they talked about, and the example of a lot of couples they've introduced us to. One of those couples has been together forty years.

Our parents are pulling for us, and that's important. I was stunned the first time Mr. Carrington stopped at our campus room and called me his son-in-law. He nearly choked on the words but it's gotten easier for him and I've learned to love it.

It's not all roses by any means, but believe me, there are enough of them to make it worthwhile. Especially when I look up from a paper on fluorescent antibody production I'm trying to wade through and see Paul smiling at me. I'm a sucker for his smile.

THE END

Other books of interest from
ALYSON PUBLICATIONS

★ ONE TEENAGER IN TEN: Writings by gay and lesbian youth, edited by Ann Heron, $4.00. One teenager in ten is gay; here, twenty-six young people tell their stories: of coming to terms with being different, of the decision how — and whether — to tell friends and parents, and what the consequences were.

★ SECOND CHANCES, by Florine De Veer, $7.00. Is it always harder to accept what is offered freely? Jeremy, who is just coming out, could easily have the love of his devoted friend Roy, yet he chooses to pursue the handsome and unpredictable Mark instead.

★ DANNY, by Margaret Sturgis, $7.00. High school teacher Tom York has a problem when the school board wants to censor many of the books he feels are most important for his classes to read. But all that pales in the face of the new difficulties that arise when he finds himself in an intense love affair with Danny, his most promising student.

★ REFLECTIONS OF A ROCK LOBSTER: A story about growing up gay, by Aaron Fricke, $6.00. When Aaron Fricke took a male date to the senior prom, no one was surprised: he'd gone to court to be able to do so, and the case had made national news. Here Aaron tells his story, and shows what gay pride can mean in a small New England town.

★ YOUNG, GAY AND PROUD, edited by Sasha Alyson, $4.00. Here is the first book ever to address the needs and problems of a mostly invisible minority: gay youth. Questions about coming out to parents and friends, about gay sexuality and health care, about finding support groups, are all answered here; and several young people tell their own stories.

★ **COMING OUT RIGHT, A handbook for the gay male,** by Wes Muchmore and William Hanson, $6.00. The first steps into the gay world — whether it's a first relationship, a first trip to a gay bar, or coming out at work — can be full of unknowns. This book will make it easier. Here is advice on all aspects of gay life for both the inexperienced and the experienced.

★ **GAY AND GRAY,** by Raymond M. Berger, $8.00. Working from questionnaires and case histories, Berger has provided the closest look ever at what it is like to be an older gay man. For some, he finds, age has brought burdens; for others, it has brought increased freedom and happiness.

★ **ACT WELL YOUR PART,** by Don Sakers, $5.00. When Keith Graff moves to a new town, he feels like the new kid who doesn't fit in. He hates his new high school and longs for familiar places and friends. Then he joins the drama club, meets the boyishly cute Bran Davenport . . . and falls in love.

★ **CODY,** by Keith Hale, $7.00. What happens when strangers meet and feel they have known one another before? When Cody and Trotsky meet in high school, they feel that closeness that goes beyond ordinary friendship — but one is straight and the other gay. Does that really matter?

★ **CHOICES,** by Nancy Toder, $8.00. This popular novel about lesbian love depicts the joy, passion, conflicts and intensity of love between women as Nancy Toder conveys the fear and confusion of a woman coming to terms with her sexual and emotional attraction to other women.

★ **THE PEARL BASTARD,** by Lillian Halegua, $4.00. Frankie is fifteen when she leaves her large, suffocating Catholic family. Here, with painful innocence and acute vision, she tells the story of her sudden entry into a harsh maturity, beginning with the man in the fine green car who does not mourn the violent death of a seagull against his windshield.

★ **A HISTORY OF SHADOWS**, by Robert C. Reinhart, $7.00. A fascinating look at gay life during the Depression, the war years, the McCarthy witchhunts, and the sixties — through the eyes of four men who were friends during those forty years.

★ **THE MEN WITH THE PINK TRIANGLE**, by Heinz Heger, $6.00. In a chapter of gay history that is only recently coming to light, thousands of homosexuals were thrown into the Nazi concentration camps along with Jews and others who failed to fit the Aryan ideal. There they were forced to wear a pink triangle so that they could be singled out for special abuse. Most perished. Heger is the only one ever to have told his full story.

★ **MEDITERRANEO**, by Tony Patrioli, $12.50. Through exquisite photos, Italian photographer Tony Patrioli explores the homoerotic territory in which, since the beginning of time, adolescent boys have discovered sex. (Oversized paperback)

★ **EIGHT DAYS A WEEK**, by Larry Duplechan, $7.00. Can Johnnie Ray Rousseau, a 22-year-old black singer, find happiness with Keith Keller, a six-foot-two blond bisexual jock who works in a bank? Will Johnnie Ray's manager ever get him on the Merv Griffin show? Who was the lead singer of the Shangri-las? And what about Snookie? Somewhere among the answers to these and other silly questions is a love story as funny, and sexy, and memorable, as any you'll ever read.

★ **IN THE TENT**, by David Rees, $6.00. Seventeen-year-old Tim realizes that he is attracted to his classmate Aaron, but, still caught up in the guilt of a Catholic upbringing, he has no idea what to do about it until a camping trip results in unexpected closeness.

★ **SOCRATES, PLATO AND GUYS LIKE ME**: Confessions of a gay schoolteacher, by Eric Rofes, $7.00. When Eric Rofes began teaching sixth grade at a conservative private school, he soon felt the strain of a split identity. Here he describes his two years of teaching from within the closet, and his difficult decision to finally come out.

★ **WORLDS APART**, edited by Camilla Decarnin, Eric Garber and Lyn Paleo, $8.00. Today's generation of science fiction writers has created a wide array of futuristic gay characters. The s-f stories collected here present adventure, romance, and excitement; and maybe some genuine alternatives for our future.

★ **SEX POSITIVE**, by Larry Uhrig, $7.00. Many of today's religious leaders condemn homosexuality, distorting Biblical passages to support their claims. But spirituality and sexuality are closely linked, writes Uhrig, and he explores the positive Biblical foundations for gay relationships.

★ **BETTER ANGEL**, by Richard Meeker, $6.00. For readers fifty years ago, *Better Angel* was one of the few positive images available of gay life. Today, it remains a touching, well-written story of a young man's gay awakening in the years between the World Wars.

These titles are available at many bookstores, or by mail.

— — — — — — — — — — — — — — — — —

Enclosed is $_____ for the following books. (Add $1.00 postage when ordering just one book; if you order two or more, we'll pay the postage.)

1. _____ 2. _____

3. _____ 4. _____

5. _____ 6. _____

name: _____ address:_____

city: _____ state: _____ zip: _____

ALYSON PUBLICATIONS
Dept. B-44, 40 Plympton St., Boston, Mass. 02118

After Dec. 31, 1990, please write for current catalog.